*Look what people are saying
about these talented authors...*

Tori Carrington

"Tori Carrington's books are noted for being sexy,
with excellent characterization and plotlines that
keep you enthralled till the very end—
and *Branded* is no different."
—*Romance Reviews Today*

"Warning needed: whatever you do—just buy the
book! Do not try to read parts in a public place!
This one is seriously, seriously passionately hot!
An absolute sizzler!"
—*freshfiction.com* on *Shameless*

"A sexy, wonderful hero, a smart, strong heroine
and a terribly interesting story combine for
a book readers won't want to put down."
—*RT Book Reviews* on *Unbridled*

Tawny Weber

"Very sexy, and with a good mystery and
well-explored characters, this is another winner."
—*RT Book Reviews* on *Going Down Hard*

"Tawny Weber's *Coming on Strong*
is a sassy, sexy tale from beginning to end
and one readers won't want to miss."
—*Romance Reviews Today*

"This book got me from the beginning....
Definitely a great read and an author that
I would want to read more of."
—*Coffee Time Romance* on *Risqué Business*

ABOUT THE AUTHORS

Bestselling authors **Lori & Tony Karayianni** are the husband-and-wife team behind the pen name Tori Carrington, and are the winners of an *RT Book Reviews* Career Achievement Award for Series Fiction. Their August 2009 Harlequin Blaze novel, *Unbridled,* marked their forty-fifth published title... and this book proves they have no plans to slow down anytime soon. Look for three books connected to this story from Harlequin Blaze later this year. For more info on the couple and their titles, and to enter their monthly online drawings, visit them at www.toricarrington.net or www.BlazeAuthors.com.

Tawny Weber is usually found dreaming up stories in her California home, surrounded by dogs, cats and kids. When she's not writing hot, spicy stories for Harlequin Blaze, she's shopping for the perfect pair of boots or drooling over Johnny Depp pictures (when her husband isn't looking, of course). Come by and visit her on the Web at www.tawnyweber.com.

Tori Carrington
Tawny Weber

BLAZING BEDTIME STORIES
VOLUME III

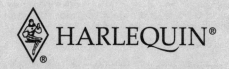

HARLEQUIN®

TORONTO • NEW YORK • LONDON
AMSTERDAM • PARIS • SYDNEY • HAMBURG
STOCKHOLM • ATHENS • TOKYO • MILAN • MADRID
PRAGUE • WARSAW • BUDAPEST • AUCKLAND

ISBN-13: 978-0-373-79517-8

BLAZING BEDTIME STORIES, VOLUME III
Copyright © 2010 by Harlequin Books S.A.

The publisher acknowledges the copyright holders of the individual works as follows:

THE BODY THAT LAUNCHED A THOUSAND SHIPS
Copyright © 2010 by Lori Karayianni and Tony Karayianni.

YOU HAVE TO KISS A LOT OF FROGS...
Copyright © 2010 by Tawny Weber.

CONTENTS

THE BODY THAT LAUNCHED A THOUSAND SHIPS

Tori Carrington

We dedicate this story to fellow
Bedtime Story lovers everywhere!

Here's hoping it fuels more than a
few sweet dreams.

And, as always, to Brenda Chin,
who is a dream editor and a great friend.

1

ONCE UPON A TIME, in a land far, far away, there was a woman on the eve of her wedding day, considering the fairy tale that was her life…

This was a dream. It had to be. At any moment, Elena Anastasios was sure her mother would poke her in the ribs to rouse her from sleep. She would wake to find herself staring at her water-stained bedroom ceiling back in their old house in Seattle, Washington, rather than taking in the exceptional sight of the large, hazy yellow sun rising over the deep blue of the Aegean Sea outside her villa window.

Elena drew in a deep breath, waiting for the poke, the pinch, the bucket of cold water that would bring her to her senses. But when she exhaled, she was still on the Greek island of Santorini. And she was still a day away from marrying one of the world's most eligible bachelors.

Lightness crowded her chest. As the only daughter of hard-working Greek-American immigrants, she'd never much believed in fairy tales. Even her mother had told her she had been the most serious girl she'd ever seen, opting to help out in the family restaurant filling napkin holders and salt and pepper shakers rather than playing with dolls.

Now she was living a fantasy. Only a year earlier she'd been worrying about how she was going to make the rent after they'd finally closed the doors on her late father's restaurant. Now she was gazing into a future that didn't hold a single monetary or, indeed, any worry at all.

After getting up and taking a quick shower, Elena pulled on a short silk robe which emphasized curves she rarely noticed she had. She slid her hands over the decadent material and shivered in anticipation. She and Manolis had yet to sleep together. Sweetly, he'd insisted that they should wait until their wedding night. She'd been okay with that. In fact, she was hoping she'd get pregnant with their first child on their honeymoon, prolonging the fairy tale element of their courtship.

Her hands stilled on her breasts and the air rushed from her lungs. If she was a little concerned that she wasn't strongly physically attracted to Manolis, she was pretty good at not thinking about it. But her small sighs of relief when he'd say good-night at the end of their dates instead of pressing for a more intimate meeting gave her away. At least to herself. Manolis thankfully didn't appear to notice.

Elena plucked her hands from her tingling flesh. Oh, so what? In her limited experience, sex was overrated. Enormously overrated. A lot of sweaty groans (on the man's part), unmet needs (on her part) and a lingering emptiness, overall, that left her wondering what all the fuss was about.

She loved Manolis. She would make sure that their sex life reflected that. And she'd invested in plenty of sexy lingerie to help her toward that end.

She smiled and stepped to the open patio doors, the view of the caldera—the sea-filled volcanic crater—stealing her thoughts away. It seemed fitting that the most important day of her life should take place in one of the most magical places on earth. If she squinted just so, it was easy to imagine Odysseus sailing the cerulean blue sea, the wisps of clouds pedestals on which Zeus and Hera stood overlooking their domain with a loving and stern hand.

Elena heard a quiet knock on her villa door and then the sound of someone using an access card to open it. She stepped back into the room and watched a young Greek maid in a crisp gray-and-white uniform duck inside carrying a plastic-covered dress and a breakfast tray.

"Good morning, miss," she said in Greek. "Your dress has been pressed, as requested." She hung the clothing on the wardrobe door and placed the tray on the bedside table.

"Thank you," Elena said, going to her purse to pull out a tip.

The maid held her hands up. "No, no. That's not necessary. *Kirio* Manolis has already well compensated all the help on the premises."

Elena wasn't surprised. Manolis was very generous. And even though he was staying on his mammoth yacht in the harbor, there was a wedding party of at least thirty people in the upscale accommodations, including Elena, her mother in the neighboring villa and her older brother.

Elena knew a moment of regret that her father wasn't there to witness the event. Regret that was no less painful now, two years after his passing.

It had been at his funeral that she'd crossed paths with wealthy Greek entrepreneur Manolis Philippidis again after having been familiar with him most of her life. She wasn't sure how her father had known him—her mother said that the two men had met shortly after immigrating to the States some thirty years earlier—but the handsome older man had proven a rock when Elena's father had suffered a massive stroke that landed him in a coma and then claimed his life shortly thereafter.

Manolis had helped look after her family financially when they'd discovered the restaurant her father had run for over twenty-five years was deep in debt, and he'd gotten her brother a job as an accountant in his extensive company's Seattle offices.

But it had been Manolis's gentle attention to Elena that had won her heart.

It also didn't hurt that her best friend, Merianna, thought he looked like a slightly younger version of a Greek Sean Connery.

"He spoils you," her mother was fond of saying. "No woman deserves the riches he lays at your feet."

"He doesn't lay anything at my feet, Mama, much less riches."

She didn't tell her mother how many extravagant gifts she'd returned to the bighearted man. Probably her mother would have insisted she give them to her instead, to stash away for a week's worth of future rainy days.

Elena wasn't sure when her warm friendship with Manolis had turned into something more. Just that the first time he'd held her, it had felt right. It hadn't mattered that he was closer to her mother's age than her own. Or that he'd been married twice already. All that was important was that for the first time in a very long time, she'd felt safe. As well as wanted.

Elena sighed wistfully as she admired the delicate pink lace of the designer cocktail dress. Tonight was the rehearsal dinner, and tomorrow she would be marrying one of the kindest men she'd ever met.

"Where would you like your breakfast, miss?" the maid asked.

Elena looked around the room. "On the patio, I think. Yes, definitely on the patio."

The maid moved the tray of rolls, coffee and orange juice to the table outside and then moved around the room almost imperceptibly, opening the curtains, fluffing pillows and smoothing the sheets.

"What's your name?" Elena asked.

"Signomi?"

Elena was glad she'd been raised in a bilingual household. It came in handy now that she was in the land of her parents. The maid had said "pardon me?", as if surprised she'd been asked a personal question.

"Pos s'lene?" she asked in Greek.

The young woman smiled, brightening her quite striking features. At maybe twenty-five or twenty-six, she was tall and quite attractive, the starched uniform doing little to disguise her soft curves and long legs. And there was something almost…regal in the way she held herself. It was a posture that Elena had been practicing, yet it appeared to come naturally to the maid.

"Aphrodite," she said.

Of course, her name would be Aphrodite. "Nice to meet you, Aphrodite. I'm Elena."

The maid's green-eyed gaze seemed to look inside her in a way that wasn't invasive but nonetheless felt a bit discomfiting.

"Is everything all right with Zaharoula?" Elena asked, wondering where the maid who had been looking after her since her arrival had disappeared to.

Aphrodite nodded. "She's fine." She gestured toward the dress. "Are you in Santorini for a special occasion?"

"Yes. I'm getting married tomorrow. To *Kirios* Philippidis."

"Congratulations," she offered. "This is a man you love?"

Elena squinted at her. Through her own familial experience, she understood that Greeks could be very forthright. But the previous maid had been little more than a phantom presence whenever she'd entered the room. This one…

Was it her, or did Aphrodite stare pointedly at the bed where only she had slept?

Elena pulled her robe around her a little more closely. "Yes. Very much."

Aphrodite disappeared into the bathroom.

Elena walked back toward the patio and picked up a croissant from the tray on the table, feeling suddenly restless. She wanted to go out. Explore the stunning island more thoroughly. Her mother claimed to be suffering from a massive attack of jetlag and had requested she not be awakened until after ten. And Lord knew what Elena's brother was doing. She leaned against the doorjamb, wondering if the locals took the mesmerizing view for granted. It was hard to imagine anyone being able to ignore the exquisite scene. She tried to make out Manolis's yacht but couldn't distinguish it from the others from a thousand feet above the sea's surface. She glanced at the brass telescope on the corner of the patio.

Movement in the water caught her attention. She shielded her eyes, watching someone swim toward a sailboat. She idly moved toward the telescope and focused it on the individual. She watched a man with rope-strong arms as he pulled himself up a ladder, water sluicing from every tanned muscle, his dark hair sleek against his head, his black swim trunks emphasizing the amazing shape he was in. He was Adonis, personified. He stood on deck and turned, shaking excess water off before picking up a thick white towel.

Elena's attention was riveted on the sight of him. Ever since arriving five days ago, she'd crossed paths with more beautiful people than she'd seen in her entire life. While the Greeks appeared to be a health- and style-conscious people, even the tourists seemed to have stepped off covers of swanky travel magazines.

The man on the boat appeared to be looking straight at her too. She hadn't noticed him lifting a pair of binoculars, as if picking up on the fact that he was being watched, and swinging his attention in her direction.

Elena's throat tightened at the thought of being caught openly ogling him. He grinned and gave a half wave. She nearly choked on the mouthful of croissant she'd been chewing and stepped back, away from the telescope and into the villa, out of sight, pretending she hadn't been looking at him.

"Aphrodite?" she called.

"Yes, Miss Elena?" the maid asked as she stepped out of the bathroom carrying used towels.

"Tell me, if I wanted to experience local life here on the island, where would I go?"

Was it her, or was there a glint in the maid's eyes?

"You have asked exactly the right person, miss…"

ARI METAXAS dropped his towel on the teak deck of the sailboat and lifted the pair of binoculars he'd been getting a great deal of use out of, sweeping the island's cliffs, looking again for the metal that the sun had glinted off. He then swung the sailboat's boom around much quicker than necessary, causing his older brother, Troy, to duck, narrowly avoiding a date with the Aegean Sea.

Troy glared at him. Ari grinned as he secured the boom. "Tell me again what the hell we're doing in Greece?"

He looked up at the villa patio, hoping to see the woman he'd spotted through the binoculars, but she was long gone. Taking her short, silky pink robe and long, tanned legs with her.

His brother turned a page of the sheaf of papers in his hands. If Troy wasn't reading a legal document of some sort, he was preparing one. It was said of the two Metaxas boys that when it came to the brain department, Troy had inherited all the genes. Ari, on the other hand, laid claim to the looks and charm.

Ari grimaced, wondering why anyone would think either of them would be happy with those descriptions. Didn't it insinuate that Troy was physically repulsive? And that Ari was as dumb as doorknob?

"We're here," Troy said in the same monotone he'd used to reply to the previous two questions Ari had asked, "because Manolis Philippidis invited us."

"Ah, that's right. The old, rich Greek guy who's getting married tomorrow, the one we're counting on and who's going to help restore Earnest, Washington to its former glory."

He felt Troy's stare again.

That hadn't come out the way Ari intended. But he couldn't help his sarcasm. It bothered him that their hometown was at the mercy of a man who was interested in only the bottom line.

Of course, had the town founders been a little more aware of the same over the past thirty years, perhaps Earnest wouldn't be suffering a twenty-five percent unemployment rate. The one-streetlight center was now little more than a ghost town with more businesses boarded up than open.

While the closing of the Metaxas lumber mill four years ago wasn't completely to blame for the town's woes, it was the most recent event.

And it was what drove Ari and his brother to try to set things right by bringing another, more solid business to the area. One with green potential. An industrial unit to develop and then produce advanced and efficient solar panels that would replace the jobs lost and hopefully create a few more.

Ari just wished that he and Troy had other prospects besides Manolis Philippidis, who had been making them jump through hoops over the past eight months with no guarantee that he would ultimately sign on the dotted line.

"What number wife is this?" Ari asked.

"Three. Now are you going to let me be so I can review these documents?"

Ari walked over to him and took the papers, slapping them onto the table nearby. "Brother, we've been in Greece for two days and I don't even think you've looked up once to see what's around you."

Troy squinted at him and then glanced around at the islands that rimmed the sea-filled caldera they were anchored in. "There, I've looked."

Ari moved the documents away from Troy when he tried to pick them back up. "Doesn't being here move you? This is the land of our forefathers. The land of Atlantis. Of Mount Olympus and Poseidon and—" he looked in the direction of the tall island cliffs a couple hundred feet away "—of Eros and Aphrodite."

Troy snatched the documents from his hands. "Yeah, I think I see all of them drinking coffee at one of those cafés over there." He sighed. "I actually met a guy named Plato this morning at a bay grocer. Then again, that shouldn't surprise me, considering our parents named you Aristotle." He shook his head as if the last thing his younger brother should have been named after was a philosopher. Ari didn't take offense. He was used to the treatment. "Look, Ari, this isn't a vacation. It's a business trip. If we finalize this deal by tomorrow, a year's worth of work will finally come to fruition." He gave a rare grin. "Then we can play."

But until then, Ari knew, he was on his own.

"So why did we lease this sailboat?" The schooner was thirty feet long and was fully loaded, including a two-man crew.

"We leased the sailboat for appearances' sake."

"Ah, right. Because Philippidis doesn't already know that our family lumber company, and by extension our town, flat-lined four years ago."

He watched his brother frown at a scribble in the margins on page twenty-two of the contract. Ari suppressed the desire to explain what the attorney had meant, that perhaps they should consider amending the paragraph on the penalty for forfeiture.

Oh, sure, he knew every last detail of the ongoing business discussions between Metaxas Limited and the Manolis Philippidis conglomerate. Not that it mattered. Troy was more than capable of taking care of things.

Which meant he had a lot of time on his hands to…

To do what, exactly?

He wished their cousin Bryna had come, but she was busy holding down the fort back home. Now *she* would have known how to enjoy her surroundings. Too bad Troy hadn't wanted to pick up the tab to bring her. So instead Ari had picked up a bunch of books and souvenirs to make her feel as if she'd been with them…

He found his gaze trailing back to the villa patio. Activity. He picked up the binoculars to find a maid cleaning the table. She looked in his direction and then straightened and smiled at him. Ari narrowed his eyes, wondering where the woman he'd spotted before had disappeared to. Then again, she could very well have been a dream, because he had the distinct impression that he wouldn't be seeing her again. Which was a shame, really. Because just looking at her had filled his mind with all kinds of ideas of things he might do with his time.

"I'm going ashore," he said suddenly, not even realizing that's what he was going to say until the words were out.

Troy barely registered his comment with a wave of his hand.

Ari went down to the cabin to change, a curious purpose to his step…

2

GIVEN THAT THE ANCIENT city of Imerovigli clung to the mountain of volcanic rock, most of the structures in the older area predated modern transportation, so there were no drivable roads, and no roads meant no cars. There was only a seemingly never-ending zigzagging line of steep, cement stairs that wound around whitewashed houses with painted shutters and colorful potted flowers, and tiny churches with blue-painted domes. Elena knew that if she turned right, she could negotiate a snaking series of wide stairs that would eventually lead to a small harbor and the water's edge. But that's not where she was interested in going this morning, especially since that's where she'd meet the skiff that would take her to the dinner on Manolis's yacht later that evening. Instead, dressed in a simple, lightweight white linen tank dress, and carrying a designer straw bag that matched her hat and sandals, she headed in the direction of the town's *agora*—the shopping district—where the locals purchased their produce.

Immediately she noticed a difference between the touristy area she was used to and the residential area, although not because the houses were any less quaint or neat. No, indeed, they appeared even more brilliant in the rising sunlight. Instead, the changes were a little less perceptible. Narrower walkways, white-painted stone pavement. And the people she encountered were more Greek. White-haired men sat playing backgammon at small tables, drinking their morning coffee, while older women in aprons swept in front of their doors or watered plants with a hose.

She nodded at the curious onlookers, offering up a Greek good morning here and there, walking on until she spotted a tented area ahead. She could virtually smell the scent of fresh lemons and peaches as she neared the area. The market bustled with the sounds of farmers hawking their wares, and locals carrying mesh bags or pushing metal carts as they bought what they would fix for dinner that afternoon.

Elena slowed her step, picking up a fig here, fingering grapes there. Although she had no practical use for the produce since she had a generous gift basket back at the villa, she bought a quarter of a kilo of each fruit and placed the bags in her purse, stepping farther on down with the crowd that seemed to move in unison in some sort of dance to unheard music.

"You do know that's an aphrodisiac, don't you?" A male voice tickled the side of her neck.

Elena drew in a deep breath. The stranger had no accent, and the aroma of limes came not from the stall of figs she stood in front of, but rather from the man she felt standing behind her.

"Really? I'd heard differently," she said in response. "They're reputed to be a great source of fiber."

A soft chuckle, then, "You're American."

"You were hoping for something else?"

She turned to face him then, nearly hitting him with the edge of her wide-brimmed hat as she did. She caught her breath for the second time as she stared into eyes the color of dark coals, noticing that his grin was as white as it was sexy.

"You're the swimmer," she said almost breathlessly.

"And you're the peeping Thomasina from the cliff…"

3

THINGS WERE VERY definitely looking up.

Having traveled widely, Ari had relatable experience to back up the saying "It's a small world." But running into the goddess he'd glimpsed on the villa patio ranked up as one of his favorite examples, if not the number one.

His grin widened.

He supposed that all depended on how the next few minutes went.

Damn, but she was beautiful. Not in the traditional sense. Her features were a little too irregular for that. Her eyes a little too wide. Her mouth a little too full. But her naturally tanned skin was smooth and flawless, her breasts full under the light tank dress, her body slamming.

Exactly the distraction he needed to fill his time.

"You're staring," she murmured, hiding under her silly, wide-brimmed hat.

"So are you." He moved to her other side when she turned, pretending an interest in the figs even though he'd watched her buy a bag earlier. "First time in Greece?"

"Actually, no."

"Do you live here?"

"No."

"Same here. On both counts."

She turned toward him and he ducked around to her other side. They were coming up toward the end of the booths and he didn't want to give her an easy escape. Not yet. Not until he'd taken his best shot and either scored…or died trying.

For reasons he couldn't quite fathom, the thought of letting her disappear into the ever-winding streets bothered him. It could be because of the somewhat fated way in which they'd come to each other's attention. Or because, frankly, the thought of returning to the sailboat and watching his brother go over papers he'd long since memorized appealed to Ari about as much as the thought of watching paint dry. So he wasn't going to let the opportunity in front of him slip through his fingers.

"Have coffee with me," he said.

She blinked as if surprised by his invitation. The darkening of her lush olive-green eyes also indicated she was intrigued.

"Listen, I'm not a guy who preys on tourists. And no, I'm not looking for a meaningless hookup." *Liar.* "I just have some free time on my hands and I can't think of anything I'd like better than to share coffee with a beautiful woman."

True enough.

"I'd like that."

SHE WASN'T DOING ANYTHING wrong, Elena silently reasoned. She was merely resting her feet after walking longer than she'd anticipated in sandals designed more for looks than comfort. She could have just as easily been seated at the romantic cliff top café by herself.

She tried to force a sip of strong Greek coffee down her throat, but it refused passage. Her body was reminding her that she wasn't by herself. She sat opposite one of the hottest men she'd ever laid eyes on.

God, she hadn't even been aware that men came in size Ari. That is what he said his name was, wasn't it? Ari? No last name. And he hadn't asked for hers.

"Let's just enjoy each other's company. Nothing more, nothing less." He'd leaned forward, meeting her halfway across the table. "You know, in case you were under the impression that I wanted to take advantage and ravish you at the first opportunity."

Elena felt her entire body go hot as she sat back in her chair. Still, she reminded herself that she wasn't doing anything to be worried about. Still, she did worry. She looked at her tiny cup, telling herself she was not disappointed that the Greeks took their coffee in small doses.

"Where else have you been in Greece?" he asked.

Elena looked up as if surprised to hear him speak. He had a nice, deep baritone voice. "Athens. Rhodes. Olympia."

"Olympia? I've never been there. I'd like to go."

The way he said it made it sound as if he'd like to go with her. Which was ridiculous. She didn't even know the man. Still, she seemed aware of him on a heightened level that was almost scary. She couldn't seem to drag her gaze away, allowing it to travel freely from his longish dark hair that her fingers itched to touch, to his generous mouth that compelled her to lick her own lips, and his wide, tanned hands that he kept visible on the table between them, the backs of his fingers peppered with dark hair that looked soft.

She cleared her throat. "You should. Visit Olympia, I mean."

His half smile seemed to indicate that he'd known what she'd been thinking…or rather, feeling. Only that was impossible.

Unless he was experiencing the same almost electric connection she was.

"Are you a swimmer?" he asked.

Elena regarded him from under her lashes. "Why do you ask?"

"You have the body of a swimmer. Long, sleek, toned."

His gaze skimmed over her body as he spoke. Elena's reaction couldn't have been more intense if he'd actually touched her. Her nipples tightened under the thin fabric of her dress, the crotch of her panties grew damp. "Um, no. I don't get much chance to swim."

"So you're from the northern States, then."

They'd agreed not to say what they were doing in Greece, or where they had come from. "Let's stick to the here and now," he'd said. She was amused that he seemed to be breaking his own rule.

"Maybe," she said.

"It wasn't a question."

"No. It wasn't."

"And you didn't ask where I was from."

She shook her head. "And I won't be asking."

Although the banter between them was tame, her reaction to it was anything but. She liked the light, playful tone of their exchange. Especially since it seemed to disguise a deeper desire to know more.

Do more.

She nervously looked at her watch. Had they already been there for twenty minutes? It seemed incredible to think the time had gone so quickly.

"Thank you for the coffee," she said, reluctant to bring the interlude to an end but knowing she didn't dare stay a minute longer.

She began to get up. He rose to his feet as if used to rising as a woman entered or exited a room. Only they weren't in a room. They were at an outdoor café.

"My pleasure," he said. "May I walk with you for a while?"

Elena's smile originated from someplace deep inside her chest. To be sure, there had been a few men in her past who had pursued her. But she'd never encouraged it. She'd never been tempted to.

But with Ari… Okay, she fully admitted that she was enjoying their harmless flirtation.

"I don't know how I could possibly stop you." She pushed the strap of her bag up to rest on her shoulder. "But I don't think it's a good idea to do it for long."

Not that she was worried about being seen with him. They were a couple of tourists taking in the magnificent sights. Nothing more. Nothing less.

She felt a pang of what she could only identity as regret. If only that was what they truly were. A couple of carefree tourists indulging in simple conversation.

But they weren't, were they? She felt anything but casual. The combination of forbidden attraction and hunger for adventure swirled together within her, prompting her to look at Ari a little more than she might have otherwise as they slowly strolled back the way they'd come, past the outdoor vegetable market, down the narrow streets.

"I wonder what this place was like a thousand years ago," Ari said as if to himself, taking in the even narrower alleyways that led off the main path.

Another time…another place…

The words echoed in Elena's mind.

"I should think it wasn't that much different," she whispered, noticing the quickening of her pulse. "Minus electricity and cell phones, that is."

He slowed his steps, forcing her to do the same as they came to another shadowy passageway. Her palms grew damp along with other more delicate areas of her anatomy. "Do you think, back then, a man who wanted to kiss a woman would do so?"

Elena's mouth seemed to fill with sand as she glanced at an old woman sitting nearby knitting, and then the other way where a man walked up the lane with a cane. But it wasn't truly their surroundings she was exploring, it was her own reaction to his suggestive question.

She wanted him to kiss her, she realized with growing anticipation and near panic.

"Right here in the open?" she whispered.

She looked to see his gaze on her, his eyes tantalizingly dark and watchful. He was pure temptation personified. "Mmm. Perhaps he might have stolen a kiss in one of these shadowy passageways."

Elena looked down the alley in question, prepared, yet unprepared when he grasped her hand and tugged her into the dark cove with him. She gasped, only to have the sound muffled by Ari's hot kiss…

ARI WAS KISSING HER. Much as he'd been longing to do for the past half hour as he sat across from her, mesmerized by her pink lips, her bedroom eyes, her supple skin, her soft curves. And the reality of pressing his mouth against hers far surpassed his fantasies.

He'd planned nothing more than a teasing peck. To pull her into the cove and sample a brief taste of her mouth. Feel the texture of his tongue against hers for a stolen moment. But as she opened up to him like a fragrant island gardenia, stretching her slender neck up so she could match his height, breathing in a labored way that found her breasts brushing against his chest every other second, his plan shattered, replaced by one far more ambitious…far more erotic.

What was it about this one woman that made him want to forget his name? Erase the reason why he was in Greece and create a completely different scenario? Forget that, although they were momentarily concealed from public view, they were still very much out in the open. But, damn it, he couldn't help himself.

He backed her against a cool wall, pressing his knee between hers until he could feel her heat against his thigh. Her mouth fell open and her eyes widened. He feared that he'd gone too far and prepared to move away from her. Had he pushed too hard? Taken things too fast?

Then her bag dropped to the pavement with a dull thud and she was pulling him to her, as caught up in the moment of reckless passion as he was.

Christ, she was beautiful. And she felt so very good pressed against him. Ari restlessly moved his hands over her, from her neck to her chest, down her outer thigh and then her inner. She deepened their kiss, the licks of her tongue growing more urgent, hungrier as she moved her head back and forth, causing her hat to fall off, her hair to tumble around her bare shoulders like silken cords.

Ari worked his fingers under the hem of her dress, pushing the fabric up, drinking in the hot, silky feel of her inner thigh with his thumb until the backs of his fingers met with the soft cotton of her panties.

He groaned at the intense need that filled him inside and out at the thought that if he wanted, he could bury his hard length in her right here, right now.

"Please," she whispered against his mouth. "I…this…"

Ari kissed her harder. Although she might be forming an objection with her words, he took comfort in the fact that her body was putty in his roving hands.

He flicked his thumb against her panties, finding the material damp from her juices, her clit stiff and swollen.

Damn…

Her fingers dug into his shoulders as if holding on for dear life, even though he had her braced against the wall with his body. One strap of her dress drooped over her shoulder and he leaned down to kiss the stretch of skin there.

She tasted like sunshine and need. And Ari couldn't get enough of her.

He urgently pushed the material of her panties aside, delving his fingers into her wet, shallow channel. She gasped and went limp in his arms, her entire body seeming to shiver with desire.

Had he ever known a woman to be so responsive? So uninhibitedly open to his advances? He couldn't have said through the fog that crowded his mind. All he could concentrate on was her and his growing need to be deep inside her.

"Please…please," she said again, shaking her head weakly. "I…can't."

Against his own wishes, Ari removed his hands from the lush garden between her legs. Her skirt instantly fell down to cover her as he cupped her face in his hands, the succulent scent of her sex filling his senses.

"Why?" he whispered, kissing her deeply.

Confusion and another emotion he couldn't immediately identify mingled with the passion on her face.

"I'm spoken for."

Then he put a name to the other emotion she exhibited: sadness.

"Sweet, beautiful Elena," he murmured, rubbing his thumbs over her high cheekbones, his gaze raking over her open mouth, her round eyes. "I'm not asking for forever. I'm asking for right now." He kissed her again. "Give it to me?"

She appeared to want to do exactly that as she strained her hips against his. Then she bit her bottom lip and looked away.

"I can give you nothing. It's not mine to give."

Ari tried to deny her escape, but her resolve forced him to step back away from her.

"I'm...sorry. So sorry," she whispered as she picked up her bag and ran away from him, her hair tangled, her mouth swollen, and the strap of her dress still dipping low over her shoulder.

4

THIS WAS CRAZY. Insane. She was a day away from marrying a good man. A very good man who loved her. Everything was arranged, guests had been flown in from all over the world. Her mother looked healthier than she had in a long time, since before her father had died.

And Elena had indulged in a wanton make out session in an alleyway with a virtual stranger.

A sinfully tempting stranger. A hungry, predatory, insatiably hot stranger.

Elena closed her eyes tightly, blocking out the fiery hues of the sun diving for the western sky. She felt the jerking of the small skiff even more acutely as it cut across the caldera on its way to *The Spartan Queen,* Manolis's well-appointed yacht.

She told herself that her uncharacteristic behavior was due to her building anticipation of her wedding night. She'd waited so long to sleep with her groom. And with one touch, she'd misdirected those emotions toward Ari.

It was also the place. She'd come down with a touch of holiday fever. Since she'd never gone on spring break with the rest of her classmates, she always guessed that their well-photographed and videotaped wild behavior was caused by the unnamed virus. The simple act of being in a foreign place, seduced by its beauty, feeling outside yourself, was to blame for uncharacteristic behavior. It was something she'd never experienced…until now.

Because never before had she done something so utterly… shameless.

Of course, she was experiencing that shame now. But she couldn't ignore that she also felt wonderfully, exhilaratingly alive.

She wished her best friend, Merianna, had been able to make the trip. She was a little more experienced in these matters. The successful attorney, who was even now tied up with an important criminal trial back in Seattle, admitted to her once that there existed taped footage of her flashing her breasts during Mardi Gras in New Orleans. She'd been nineteen at the time, Merianna had bemoaned, and she'd had a few drinks. Now she spent many a late night praying that no one at the law firm ever came across it.

"That's more like it," her mother said.

Elena looked at the woman standing next to her. "What is?"

"You're smiling."

"Why wouldn't I be?"

"Well, you haven't been doing a whole lot of it since we left Washington."

Elena grasped the side of the boat when they hit a wake left by a speedboat. "Of course I have."

"No, you haven't. You looked like you were going to your death instead of getting married."

Had she? Elena turned her head to stare back out at the impossibly blue sea. Could what her mother said be true? Had she not smiled?

And if she was smiling now, what was the cause?

Ari…

She refused to believe it. She was getting married tomorrow. In this lovely place. To a marvelous man. She was on top of the world.

And happy that she had known the taste of Ari's lips, if only for a brief moment. A snip in time that no one else had to know about. Her husband would be reaping the rest of the benefits from here on out.

Her smile widened and she closed her eyes, allowing the sun to wash her face in golden light.

"FOR A GUY WHO DIDN'T want to go to this thing earlier, you're in an awful hurry to get there now," Troy said, checking his cufflinks while he and Ari waited for the skiff that would ferry them the thirty feet to Manolis Philippidis's yacht *The Spartan Queen.*

Ari grinned unabashedly. "The sooner we're there, the sooner we can leave."

"I knew you had to have an ulterior motive." Troy smacked him on the shoulder. "Thanks for doing this."

"No need for thanks. We're in this together."

Troy looked out over the Aegean, though Ari suspected he didn't see a drop of it. "Yes, well, sometimes I wonder about that."

Ari squinted against the sunlight that bounced off the sparkling waves. "If that's the case, then I apologize. It was never my intention."

He felt a twinge of guilt. Not because of his involvement, or lack thereof, in the company's current business affairs. Troy had never wanted or needed his help beyond what he asked him to do. Ari hated going over the same numbers and contracts again and again. The way he saw it, you nailed something down and moved on. You didn't debate it to death. It was either right or it was wrong. There was no room for middle ground or doubt.

His brother was more than capable of taking care of the contract end of things. And Ari had no intention of being a second cook in the kitchen.

No, the guilt he felt was because he wasn't being entirely honest with his brother. Oh, he had every intention of leaving this party early. Far earlier than Troy could imagine. Because he had a woman to seek out. And he intended to begin that search as soon as possible.

"Here we are," Troy said, indicating Ari should board the skiff first.

Ari did so, his eyes trained on the high cliffs behind them. Was she there in her villa? And if she was, was she scanning the sea looking for him, as he searched for her?

He grinned. Ah, yes. He was going to be leaving this party as soon as he arrived…

"ELENA, WHERE ARE YOU?"

Elena blinked her mother's face into view. Where was she? She was standing on the first deck of a four-deck megayacht next to her groom-to-be in the middle of dozens and dozens of people she didn't know, her groom at her left elbow, her mother at her right, a little less than a half of a day away from her wedding.

She'd been on the four-hundred-foot yacht before, but then it had been easy to deceive herself into thinking that only the one deck existed, only the one cozy cabin. But with countless guests arriving in their sparkling best, and disappearing somewhere on the yacht, white-clad servers offering up flutes of champagne and trays of fancy hors d'oeuvres, a live if abbreviated orchestra playing, she felt almost lightheaded.

Then again, maybe it was the champagne. Before she'd realized it, she'd downed one glass and was well into her second. And, if she wasn't mistaken, the yacht was no longer anchored.

"Carlo! Come here. I want you to meet my lovely bride-to-be, Elena," Manolis said, putting his arm around her waist.

As she had a number of times already, she smiled and extended her hand to another Mediterranean older man with a younger woman on his arm. She'd made the mistake of referring to one as the man's wife when apparently she'd been his mistress, so she'd stopped asking personal questions.

She pulled at her dress, wondering why it suddenly felt too tight, when just a short time ago it had fit perfectly.

There were too many people, and none of them were family, save her own. She'd hoped to meet Manolis's adult children from a previous marriage, but he'd told her tonight that they wouldn't be attending. As for his mother, and siblings, he'd said Elena would meet them at the ceremony tomorrow.

The only people close to him that she knew were his ever-present Greek bodyguard, Gregoris, who towered over her by a foot and made her uneasy whenever he looked her way, and Caleb, one of the top executives of his multinational company, a man who couldn't be much older than she was and who always had a different woman on his arm.

"Eat something," her mother said, holding a plate of hors d'oeuvres in front of her.

Elena gently pushed it away. "We're going to be sitting down for dinner soon."

Where were they going to fit all these people? She noticed the event and wedding planner moving through the room. She should ask if everything was under control. Unfortunately, she calculated that by the time she reached where the planner was now, the other woman would be long gone.

"Are you all right, darling?" Manolis asked.

Elena smiled at him and nodded. "Fine. I'm fine. Do you think we have enough tables for everyone?"

Manolis smiled and held her a little closer to his side. "Everything's taken care of. There's nothing you need to worry your pretty little head about."

Elena resisted making a face, even as she laid her finger on exactly what was bothering her—she wasn't used to being the pretty little head in any situation. Since her father had died, she had become more accustomed to being the organizer than the one hiring the organizer.

That was okay. She'd just have to adjust, that's all. Besides, she didn't think they'd be hosting such a large event again anytime soon. She'd have plenty of time before the next one to get her bearings.

She took a sip from her champagne flute again then realized she hadn't intended to. Water. She needed some water.

"Are you ready?" Manolis asked her, his hand on her shoulder.

Her breath rushed from her. She hadn't known how much she'd wanted to hear that question until he'd asked it. It was all so confusing. Overwhelming. She wasn't sure if she was ready.

She opened her mouth to speak when she realized that he wasn't asking her if she was ready to get married, but if she was ready for dinner.

"Mr. Philippidis. Thanks so much for inviting us. You have a phenomenal craft."

Manolis turned toward the male voice. It belonged to a man Elena didn't recognize but one who looked somewhat familiar.

"Mr. Metaxas. Thank you for coming. I'm glad you could make it." Manolis shook his hand.

"You remember my brother, Ari, don't you?"

Elena's heart skipped a beat at the sound of the name. And then stopped altogether when the man stepped aside, revealing the one person she'd never expected to see again.

HEY, HEY, HEY. Looked like he wasn't going to have to go searching for his dream girl after all.

Ari grinned widely. Talk about kismet. He'd come to the event so he could duck out, only to find what he was looking for right, smack dab in front of him.

"Of course, I remember Ari," Manolis Philippidis was saying as he shook his hand. "I don't think you've had the pleasure of meeting my intended, Elena."

Ari's hand dropped like a stone to his side. Had Manolis just said what he thought he had?

He suspected he was staring at her in much the same way she was staring at him, with an expression that could only be described as a bad impression of a grouper.

She was Philippidis's trophy-wife-to-be? It wasn't possible. How, with all the tourists and locals inhabiting the Aegean island, had he met and become infatuated with the one woman off limits to him?

He felt Troy's elbow in his side. "Ari?"

He realized Manolis was eyeing him suspiciously.

"Have you met my bride-to-be already, then?" Manolis asked.

Ari looked at him and smiled coolly. "No. No, I have not. If I had, I'm sure I would have remembered." He turned back to Elena, forcing himself to breathe as he raised her hand and kissed it. "Her beauty has rendered me speechless, I'm afraid."

Manolis beamed proudly, Ari's brother, Troy, sighed in relief and Elena tugged her hand back with more force than was necessary.

"Come, come," Manolis said, waving for them to follow him. "We're just sitting down to dinner. I'd like it if you'd sit at our table."

Elena flashed him a look of panic, as if pleading with him to refuse.

"We'd be honored," Ari said instead.

She couldn't breathe.

Elena made her way out to the side deck, somewhere, anywhere there were few people. The past hour had been a study in patience as she sat two chairs away from Ari and endured the ceaseless smoky looks he'd sent her way, making her feel so hot she was afraid her dress would spontaneously combust.

She'd never been so relieved when Manolis had wished her a good night, excusing himself and several of his male guests as they retired to enjoy cognac and a cigar and talk shop, leaving her on her own for the rest of the evening.

"Elena?"

She swung around to face her mother.

"What's the matter, *agape mou?*" she asked, referring to her as "my love."

She tried for a smile. "I don't know. I just needed to get some air."

And what air it was. Fresh and fragrant, the salt of the sea coating her lips.

Ekaterina moved next to her and they stood side by side staring out at the rising moon. "Every bride gets cold feet."

Elena tightened her grip on the top rail. "I don't have cold feet."

She didn't, did she?

She recalled her earlier thoughts about everything moving too quickly. "It's just that…" She looked at her mother. "Don't you find all of this…overwhelming? So much…wealth. So much material possession. I mean, I knew Manolis was rich, but I don't think I understood just how rich until now."

"And that is a bad thing?"

Elena laughed. "I know, it sounds stupid, doesn't it?"

Her mother put an arm around her. "Not stupid...oh, okay. Maybe it does sound a little bit naive."

Naive. Now that's a word she had never been called. Which meant this was a day of firsts for her. Not the least of which was her unexpected attraction to a man not her intended.

"I'm going back in," her mother said. "You should come with me."

Elena nodded but didn't budge.

"Don't be too long."

"I won't," she promised.

She just needed a few more moments to try and wrap her head around everything.

Elena closed her eyes tightly as she listened to her mother's footsteps retreat then she drew in a deep breath. Everything had seemed to happen so naturally. One event led to the next and then to the one after that.

So why was she suddenly experiencing such a deep and full case of the doubts? Could it be the cold feet her mother had talked about? Was it true that all brides went through the worry she was experiencing? That after tomorrow all would be well and bright?

She couldn't imagine everything being right again. Only different. Terrifyingly different.

"Here I spent the past hour wondering how I was going to get you alone," a male voice said a little too close to her ear. "And you went and solved the dilemma for me..."

Why did she have the icy certainty that this was but the beginning of a dilemma no one would be able to solve for her?

5

DAMN, BUT SHE WAS even sexier than he remembered. And that was nearly impossible, because he'd already built her up to impossible proportions in his mind all afternoon, ever since their parting near the outdoor market.

Ari let his gaze trail over her bare shoulder, down her arm and then to her rounded bottom. Even her slender ankles seemed to beg him for attention. And it was all too easy to imagine them crossed behind his back, those decadent lips of her parted in ecstasy.

Elena quickly turned, interrupting his perusal.

"What are you doing?" she whispered urgently, looking both ways up the deck, though no one was there; the guests were too busy enjoying dessert in the five-course dinner service. "Someone could see you."

He moved closer yet, her scent filling his senses. An intoxicating mix of gardenia oil and sea air. As much as she tried to pretend that his presence on the yacht didn't move her, he could tell that she was just as aware of his proximity as he was of hers. It was as if every move seemed to take forever. Every gaze lingered for an hour. Every heartbeat echoed in his ears, making it impossible to concentrate on casual conversation over the thundering racket.

He wanted her. Badly.

It was as simple and as complicated as that.

He wanted her and he intended to have her. Wealthy grooms, angry brothers and the entire world be damned.

"Please don't look at me that way." Her voice was barely audible and made his hard-on ache beneath the fabric of his tux pants.

"Why?"

"Because I can't think when you do."

Honesty. He liked that. "The way I figure it, it's only fair that you feel the same as I do."

"You don't even know me."

"Mmm, nor you me. But that didn't stop what passed between us earlier in town."

She looked away, and he was pretty sure she blushed, although it was difficult to tell in the dim light.

"I want to finish it," he murmured.

She gasped, her eyes wide. "I'm getting married tomorrow."

"And that affects me how?"

"Correct me if I'm wrong, but judging from dinner conversation, you and your brother are trying to close a business deal with Manolis."

"Yes, and we're standing on a 405-foot megayacht that is worth ten times the investment we're asking for."

"How do you think he'll react when he finds out you're stalking his fiancée?"

Ari hiked a brow. He'd been called a lot of things, but he'd never been accused of being a stalker.

"Is that what you think I'm doing?"

"It is, isn't it? Your following me out here like this. Earlier in town."

"I'm trying to seduce you, Elena. There's a difference.

And I think you understand that because I get the definite impression that you want to be seduced."

She appeared not to know what to say.

"All you have to do is tell me to go away, Elena."

He didn't miss her shiver. "Go away," she whispered.

He tsked. "You'll have to do better than that."

"Go away," she tried again, this time sounding a little more convincing.

"Or else?"

"Or else I'll…I'll…"

"You'll scream and alert the entire guest list, including your groom?"

She tried to move past him. He knew instant fear that he might never stand this close to her again. The feeling was so engulfing, so shocking, that he kicked into what he could only call instinct mode and grasped her arm.

"Let me go."

Ari grinned at her, a plan unraveling in his mind.

In one smooth move, he scooped her up, one arm behind her shoulders, the other under her knees. She gasped, grabbing on to him to keep from falling.

"Let me down!"

"Happy to oblige." He lifted her out over the rail and did exactly as she asked.

ELENA'S MOUTH and throat filled with water as she swam for the surface. He'd thrown her overboard! She broke the surface and sputtered, coughing as she kicked in her high heels, her dress weighing her down. She searched for a point of reference in the dim light from the moon, finding herself next to the yacht, the first deck railing a good twenty feet above her.

"Make way!"

Elena gasped as Ari landed in the water next to her. She swirled one way, then other, searching for him. He popped up behind her, instantly curving an arm around her ribcage.

"What do you think you're doing?" She tried to wriggle free of his grasp.

"Why, I'm saving you, of course."

"Saving me? You're the one who threw me into the damn water to begin with!"

"No, I didn't. Hold still."

"Hold still for what?"

"So I can save you."

"Will you stop saying that. It's thanks to you that I'm in here at all." She tried to pry his fingers from her waist. "Let... me...go."

She clamped her mouth shut, realizing those very words had gotten her into trouble in the first place. She needed to be very careful what she said to Mr. Ari Metaxas. She could seal her fate without ever realizing she'd done so.

Even as she protested, she couldn't help reacting to his damp closeness. His body heat burned as hot as any fire, seeping through her wet clothes. She also felt a certain other body part pressing into her backside, a fact that wasn't altogether unpleasant.

Unpleasant? The thought that he was turned on by current events both enraged and excited her. The water was cool, but not uncomfortably so. The taste of the salt on her lips ignited a hunger that dinner a short time ago had been unable to accomplish.

"Oh, God," she said.

"What? Are you all right?"

"I can't go back like this." She'd gone to such great pains to make herself attractive tonight. What did she say when they swam around the back, guests looking on as she climbed from the water looking like a drowned rat, her hair a matted mess, her makeup smeared and running, her dress in ruins?

"Well, good thing we're not going back, then."

"What?" She realized she was helping him swim and stopped. "Didn't you just say that you couldn't go back like this?"

"Yes, but—"

"I've already adjusted for the possibility."

She noticed the yacht was getting farther away, not nearer, as Ari held on to her with one strong arm, and stroked water with the other.

"Where are you taking me?" She knew alarm. They could easily get lost in the inky darkness and drown. She opened her mouth to scream, praying someone would hear her over the music on the yacht, but found herself being pulled under water when she tried.

She spat out the liquid that filled her mouth.

"Sorry," Ari murmured in her ear.

She hit at his arm. "You are not sorry! You're kidnapping me."

"Hmm. I hadn't thought about it that way, but I guess I am."

"Let…me…go." She renewed her struggle against him.

He couldn't kidnap her! She was getting married tomorrow.

"Stop or you'll drown us both," he warned ominously, spitting out a mouthful of water.

Elena stopped struggling. He was right. Whatever he had planned, she could deal with it when they were in safer territory. The middle of the Aegean at night was not the place to wage war.

The problem was, that if she wasn't fighting him, it was all too easy to lean into him. And she absolutely, positively refused to do that. While she might be suffering from a major case of cold feet, she still had a pretty good idea where she wanted those feet to be. And it wasn't wherever Ari's were.

"Here. Let me help you up."

She blinked as he guided her hands to grip something solid. It was the sailboat she'd seen him on earlier. Surely there was a crew on board? And definitely a satellite phone. She could use either one to find her way back to familiar territory.

She felt his hand curve under her bottom, and he boosted her up onto the ladder. Once on deck, she turned and considered kicking him back overboard. If only that would keep him from climbing up again.

"You're insane," she said when he stood next to her, dripping water from his tux shirt and pants. She realized he must have shrugged out of his jacket at some point. Before or after he'd joined her in the sea? She didn't know.

What she did know was that she was cold.

"Come here."

She hugged herself tightly and refused to look at him.

"Fine then. Be stubborn."

He came up from behind her and draped a thick, dry towel around her shoulders. Elena clutched it in relief. Was she really still wearing her heels? Shit, she should have gone ahead and kicked him while he was on the ladder. Maybe she'd have done some damage.

She reached down and slid each ruined designer shoe off until she stood in her bare feet.

"How much are you going to ask for?" she asked, running the towel over her hair and trying to gauge how far away the yacht was. So close, yet so far. She could make out the tinny strains of the orchestra. Was that really "Strangers in the Night"? She shook her head, wondering if anyone had missed her yet. How long would it take them to figure out she wasn't on board?

She stalked toward the cabin steps. Before she'd moved two feet, Ari stopped her with a hand on her upper arm.

"Where do you think you're going?"

"To ask the crew for help."

"There is no crew."

She glared at him.

"They're all on shore for the night."

"Liar."

He released her. "Go and check for yourself."

She did.

She went belowdecks, the recessed lighting making her progress swift as she checked four sleeping quarters, all empty.

Of course. The crew wouldn't be where they could mingle with the guests.

She emerged onto the deck and made her way to the stern. Sure enough, there was another set of stairs. Only the additional four cabins and galley she found there were also empty.

She leaned against the counter and closed her eyes. What was she going to do?

Phone. A satellite phone.

She crouched and began looking through the cabinets, and then moved to what looked like a small navigational room. They had to have a satellite phone somewhere for backup in case a storm kicked up.

She emerged onto the deck again and made her way to the bow. Bingo. A radio. Surely she could raise someone on it. The crew on *The Spartan Queen* would be ideal.

She picked up the handset and began flicking buttons.

"Mayday, mayday," she said into the mouthpiece, unsure if she was broadcasting as she continued to press, pull and flick.

The tail of the phone cord hit her hip. She picked it up to find it wasn't plugged in.

Or, rather, someone had just unplugged it.

She turned to find Ari leaning against the foremast, considering her. He'd taken off his shirt and shoes and his dark eyes glistened amusingly and somewhat dangerously.

"Do you really want to see me arrested?" he asked.

She squinted at him. "Are you serious?"

"Deathly. Have you ever seen *Midnight Express?*"

She gave an eye roll at his mention of the film in which an American student is sent to a Turkish prison for trying to smuggle drugs. "That was Turkey. Not Greece."

"And the difference?"

She was sure there was some, but was also equally sure that the prisons here would probably make the ones back home look like luxury resorts.

She put the handset back where it belonged and crossed her arms. "I'll make you a deal—you get me back to shore and no one has to know about…well, the fact that you've kidnapped me." She made a face. "How much of a ransom were you planning to ask for, anyway?"

He chuckled, the sound echoing on the waves. He pushed away from the mast and came to stand in front of her, using a corner of the towel around her to wipe her cheeks. Elena knew she should stop him, step away, anything but allow the intimate gesture, but she was glued to the spot, watching him.

"Money isn't everything, my dear Elena," he murmured, his gaze on her mouth. "In fact, there are things of much greater value to be had."

Her throat tightened to the point of pain. "Such as?"

He leaned in and kissed her. "This…"

6

Ari slid his mouth over hers, kissing her lightly, lingeringly. She tasted of the sea and pure temptation. He lifted his fingers to her cheek and then reached behind her head to tug at the pearl pins there until the dark cloud of her hair floated around her shoulders in wet ringlets.

She made a soft sound of pleasure, making him realize that if he wanted to, he could take her right then and there. Slide his hand up her dress and stroke her to the point of sheer neediness. And, oh, how he wanted to do just that. But he knew that the instant the heat of their passion cooled, she'd be at the same place she was five minutes ago, desperately trying to escape him and running back to a well-planned life with Manolis Philippidis.

He didn't want that. He wanted her to be moved by their joining. To inspire her to gaze at the alternate future stretching ahead of her. One that hopefully included him.

The thoughts should have surprised him. And in a distant way, they did. But since their alleyway exchange, he'd burned with a desire to not only know her carnally, but in every way it was possible for a man to know a woman. And that was well before he knew of her engagement.

Ari ended the kiss and drew a deep breath. "Why do I get the feeling you're going to be the end of me?"

She restlessly licked her lips as if hoping he would continue. Which is exactly where he wanted her to be. For now.

"I have a proposition to make."

She stared at him for a long moment and then began to move away.

"No, no, hear me out before you pass judgment."

The sound of the thick click of her swallow was stolen by the light breeze. "Please, don't let me stop you," she said. "I certainly haven't been able to stop you from doing anything you've wanted so far."

He groaned. This is not where he wanted her to be. "Granted, the kidnapping part might not have been such a great idea…"

She moved a step back and crossed her arms. "That's putting it mildly."

"But even you have to admit that there's…something between us, Elena. Something elemental. Powerful."

She sucked her bottom lip between her teeth.

"We're not teenagers, so this isn't a crush. Or a holiday fling type of thing…"

Her eyes widened. Had she been considering the same explanations he had? Trying to make sense out of what was happening between them?

"My request is this—give us one night. Tonight. If this is only about sex, then we'll both wake up in the morning and continue on with our lives as if it never happened."

"And my life will be ruined. And so, quite plausibly, will yours."

He flashed her a grin. "Nobody ever has to know. Admit it. You won't be missed on the yacht. Not tonight. The men had already retired to do their best Masters of the Universe impressions, so I assume Manolis had already said good-night."

She looked off in the distance.

"And the rest of the guests will assume that you're busy elsewhere."

"My mother…"

"It will be easy to convince your mother that you weren't feeling well and went back to the island early, to prepare for tomorrow's activities." She looked at him. "Yes, I heard your conversation."

This appeared to upset her. Why, he wondered? Because he had overheard a private conversation? Or because she had expressed doubt about marrying a man twice her age?

Either way, he steered the subject back to calmer waters.

"And if we wake up in the morning to discover it isn't strictly about the sex…?"

Ari rubbed his chin with his index finger. "Well, that's something we owe it to ourselves to find out, isn't it? But we can't do that unless we actually…have sex."

There. There it was. He'd placed his cards on the table. It was up to her to decide whether or not he held a winning hand.

He watched as she paced one way and then the other, appearing to consider his proposition.

"Is that it?" she asked.

"I'm sorry? I'm not sure I know what you mean."

"That's the best you can do?"

Ari winced inwardly. He'd been called out. And he had no idea how to respond.

"Okay."

He blinked. "What?"

Her smile was wide and bright. "I said, 'okay.'" She looked around. "Where can I shower?"

ELENA HAD ABSOLUTELY no idea what she was doing. But it didn't look like she was going to be getting off this boat anytime soon. And there was that little matter of the desire pulsing in her veins. It wasn't such a bad idea to see what, if anything, would happen, if she just this once gave herself over to pure human impulse rather than rational thought.

She finished drying off from her shower and stood in front of the steam-covered mirror, considering her reflection. It seemed appropriate somehow that her image was blurry. She felt blurry. Unsure of the daring woman staring back at her. She had no makeup, she had no sexy lingerie, but that didn't matter. She looked around the small bathroom and found a man's white shirt hanging on the back of the door. She smelled the sleeve, detecting the scent of Ari's cologne. Sandalwood and lime. She shrugged into the shirt and did up the buttons, and then undid them again, leaving only two barely holding the material together at her midsection.

She took a deep breath and leaned against the door. What was she doing? To invite this man into her life was nothing short of insane. But that hadn't stopped her from acting like a hungry wanton earlier that day. What made that person different from the one she was now? Very little. Except that she was that much closer to exchanging vows with another man.

But she wasn't married yet, a small, insistent voice whispered.

And if she went through with this night, she might never marry.

She refused to think about that now. She'd made up her mind and nothing was going to change it.

She quickly pulled open the door, startling Ari where he stood on the other side. Behind him, the cabin's double bed had been turned down, the pillows fluffed.

She fought a smile.

"Uh, hi," he said.

Was it her, or did he appear nervous?

Strange. He'd spent so much of the past hour trying to convince her to sleep with him, and now that she'd agreed, it seemed that he didn't know what to do.

It was wonderfully appealing.

She stepped into the cabin and noted the other things he'd done: the brighter lights had been switched off, leaving one small mounted lamp above the headboard to create a golden circle on the wall.

She stepped forward.

Ari stepped back.

"Are you hungry?" he asked.

She was taken aback. "Pardon me?"

He ran his hand through his dark hair. "It's just that I noticed you hadn't eaten much earlier and I thought you might be hungry. I could, um, fix us an omelet or something light…"

Elena moved closer to him…and he moved back.

She nearly laughed at the ridiculousness of it all. If only it wasn't so empowering to know that she had this kind of effect on him.

She'd never been the type of girl construction workers whistled at. Or the kind that high school boys stuttered around. Is this what it felt like? Maybe she should have worn tighter tops, brighter colors. Because this was nice.

More than nice, it was a turn-on unlike anything she'd ever experienced.

"Actually, I am hungry," she murmured, stepping even closer, until his legs hit the bed, leaving him nowhere else to go. Elena rubbed the tip of her nose against the glorious line of his jaw and inhaled deeply. "But it's not food I'm craving."

He chuckled, minus his usual bravado. "Funny. That's funny."

She met his gaze, their faces mere inches apart. "I'm not laughing."

He cleared his throat. "No, you're not, are you?"

"Uh-uh." She slowly shook her head.

Ari's pupils widened as he eyed her mouth. "So, um, what do we do now?"

Elena raised her hands to his bare chest. He was hot. Literally. His skin felt like heated satin over titanium. She allowed herself a few brief moments of indulged touching, and then shoved him to the bed.

"How about we start here and see what happens…"

IT WAS SO NOT THE WAY he saw this going down.

Ari wasn't sure what had happened, but in the time Elena had taken showering, he'd started to doubt himself.

Was it possible that he never expected her to accept the terms of his offer? That he'd seen a fight coming instead of his fantasy of having this hungry cat climbing onto the bed, placing her bare knees on either side of his hips, her dark eyes glistening.

Maybe it was performance anxiety. Not that he'd know what that felt like, because it had certainly never happened to him before. But considering who Elena was, and how much he'd built up his own prowess, could he be, on some blasted subconscious level, afraid he couldn't live up to his own hype?

Hype? He'd never misrepresented himself in any situation. Ever.

Kiss her, you fool.

He leaned in, claiming her naked lips with his. She smelled of his soap, which was even better on her. He silently groaned and turned his head, at the same time she turned hers. They bumped noses.

"Ow."

"Sorry," he murmured.

He went in again and tried to swivel her toward the bed. Her heel hit his big toe just right.

"Ouch."

"Sorry."

He felt his way down the front of the shirt she wore, sliding his hand inside. Soft, so soft. He budged his fingers toward her right breast, cupping the full mound, finding the tip stiff and thick. He lightly pinched the flesh and she muttered another "ow."

Ari stepped back and stared at her. "This isn't exactly going right, is it?"

She gave a relieved laugh. "No, it isn't."

He ran his hands over his hair a couple of times, trying to come to grips with the awkwardness of the moment.

He wanted this woman. More than he could remember wanting anyone else.

Why, then, the problems?

He looked down to his pants front. Pericles wasn't having any trouble at all. He was so hard it almost hurt.

"What's say we try this again," he offered.

Elena nodded and then licked her lips.

"Wait," he said, when she moved to step closer. "What's say we move on to step two?"

The thought of seeing her totally nude made him harder still. He reached for the shirtfront and easily undid the two fastened buttons. The fabric opened enough for him to see the long, tanned line of her stomach and half her breasts, but left everything covered.

Whatever hesitation he felt vaporized as pure, consuming need gripped him. In that moment, he didn't fear what might happen, didn't wonder whether or not his performance would fall short. All he wanted was to make love to this strikingly beautiful woman, claim her, brand her with his hands and his mouth.

He slowly pushed the fabric back over her shoulders. The shirt whooshed from her and pooled in a white puddle at her feet even as she unzipped his pants. They instantly fell to his ankles, revealing that he wasn't wearing underwear either.

Her eyes widened as she took in his highly aroused state.

Ari grinned. Oh, yes. This was much more like it...

He backed her toward the bed and she tumbled down, scooting farther back with her knees together, leaning toward one side. He stepped to the edge of the bed and ran his hands over her shins and knees, bringing them up. Then, with his gaze melded to hers, he slowly opened her thighs, baring the most intimate parts of herself to him.

Ari's heart beat a thick rhythm in his chest as he took in the dark, springy curls. He moved his hands inward, sliding them, reveling in the feel of her even as he breathed in her unique, sweet musky scent. His mouth watered as he knelt on the bed and pushed her upward still. He leaned inward and kissed her deeply, only their mouths touching. He kissed her, and kissed her again, until her breathing came in ragged gasps and her breasts trembled with need. Then he reluctantly broke the contact and licked his way down each of her breasts, suckling the puckered bits, before continuing farther.

The instant his mouth touched her curls, her back came up off the bed. Ari splayed one hand against her stomach, holding her still, even as he parted her with his other. She opened like a ripe fig, pink and juicy and mouth-watering.

He dipped his tongue in the shallow channel and brought

it up, running the very tip around the tight bud at the top. Then he fastened his mouth around it and suckled gently.

Her cry as she achieved orgasm was worth a hundred sore toes…

7

Elena couldn't catch her breath. Her fists were still entangled in the sheets, Ari was still between her legs and all she could manage were choking gasps.

"I...you...never...can't...this..." she rasped incoherently as she attempted to drag massive amounts of air into her lungs.

There wasn't a part of her that didn't feel the earthquake that had rocked her body. No one had ever gone down on her before. One date had tried, but she'd been too shy to allow it.

What in the hell had she been thinking?

Ari continued his delicate lapping. She let go of the sheet and threaded her fingers through his hair. Look at her! She was trembling all over.

Finally, he lifted his head to look at her, his eyes drawing her into their dark depths. She welcomed his weight against her as he shifted until they were nose-to-nose, her arms encircling his waist and her palms running along the muscles of his back and down to his backside.

What a phenomenal male specimen he was. Perfect in every way. No Greek god had anything on Ari Metaxas. He could easily have been the model on which artists had based their work. His arms were strong, his chest broad, his waist narrow, his thighs thick.

Then there was what lay between his legs.

Elena reached for him. She could barely get her fingers around his width, and his length made her wonder if she could possibly handle it all.

She restlessly licked her lips in between kisses. She didn't know, but, oh boy, did she ever want to try.

She spread her thighs wider and his erection instantly pressed lengthwise against her aching sex. Oh how she wanted this man. In a hungry, unabashed, uninhibited way that might have frightened her if she'd been capable of thinking at all. But she wasn't, so she didn't.

His tongue caressed hers with slow deliberation, but she was so impatient to have him inside her that she wriggled, trying to force entry. When that didn't work, she reached between them again, positioning his burgeoning head against her and bearing upward.

Oh, yes, oh, yes, oh, yes, oh yes…

Her blood seemed to rise up toward her heart, giving her a curious full feeling. And he had yet to completely enter her. What would happen when he did?

Instead he withdrew.

No, no, no, no…

He entered her again and every molecule of air left her lungs as he slid in to the hilt in one, long, magnificent stroke.

Yes…

Elena felt wondrously, gloriously alive, as if her heart was the size of her entire body.

So this was what sex, good sex, was supposed to be like. She'd…had…no…idea.

"Look at me," Ari said huskily.

Elena opened her eyes, seeing the way she felt reflected in his tight-jawed expression. Exquisite pleasure rippled through her at the sight of him stroking her inside and out. So feral, so natural, so damn beautiful.

To her amazement, she found a sob gathering in her throat. She opened her eyes wide even as they filled with tears.

Ari slowed.

"No! Oh, God, please no," she rasped.

He not only continued his thrusts, he increased the urgency of each, hitting spots she'd never been formally introduced to, much less knew well. She clutched his shoulders, trying to anchor herself, yet urging him to come along with her for the ride. It was like she was being propelled through some fog-misted, lush wonderland full of vivid colors and sweet aromas.

Then it all shattered, leaving her feeling as if she lay in a thousand, explosive pieces throughout the cabin…

ARI COULDN'T REMEMBER a time when he'd been so sore following sex. His balls felt empty. Pericles was raw. His muscles ached as if he'd just completed a marathon. Yet, miraculously, he felt energized rather than exhausted. As if he could spend the rest of the day making love to Elena just as they had spent the entire night.

If he didn't know better, he'd think it was the first time she'd ever achieved climax during sex. She was at turns surprised and wantonly curious, bursting into tears now and again, insisting that they weren't born of sadness but joy.

He finished shaving and opened the bathroom door. Elena was spilled across his bed facedown, deep asleep, one long leg poking out of the sheet along with an arm. He made out the curve of a luscious breast. As if on command, Pericles twitched in his white linen pants.

Down, boy, he insisted. While he knew that all he had to do was kiss Elena and she'd welcome him back to bed, he needed sustenance before he could even consider making love to her again.

He also needed to make sure that there wasn't a search party out looking for the woman who had rocked his night.

He gripped the handrail and took the stairs two at a time, emerging from the cabin and into the bright morning sun. He blinked several times.

"What time is it?"

He wasn't surprised to find Troy already enjoying breakfast at the nearby table, going over yet more columns of numbers positioned next to his plate.

"Nine."

Ari picked up his glass of orange juice and drained it.

"Hey," his brother complained. "Get your own."

"What time did you get out of there last night?"

"Late. What time did you duck out?"

"Early."

Ari liberated a piece of toast from the small stack. So Troy thought he'd gone into town. He was also fairly sure that his brother wouldn't be sitting there calmly eating breakfast if he knew the truth: that Ari had essentially kidnapped the bride-to-be and that even now, she was asleep in his bed.

"I made great progress last night," Troy said, turning the page. "We're a pen stroke away from getting everything we want." He frowned. "Or nearly everything. The old man drives a hard bargain."

Ari's gut tightened. "That's nice."

If his response sounded hollow, Troy apparently hadn't noticed.

"Manolis has invited us to bring the final contracts to the pre-ceremony luncheon." His brother consulted the laptop at his other elbow. "I'm getting everything ready now." He finally looked up at Ari. "I'd appreciate it if you were there."

One of the crewmembers approached, offering Ari breakfast. He accepted, and then added, "Make it full fare for two."

Troy grimaced. "I already have mine."

"Who says it's for you?"

His brother's hand paused where he typed. "You brought a girl back to the boat? That's unlike you, Ari."

"Yes, well, I've been doing a lot of unusual things lately," he said quietly, stepping to the edge of the deck and staring out at the stunning, postcard-perfect view.

How could he explain to his brother that the wedding wasn't going to happen? And that once the groom-to-be discovered the reason why, it was highly unlikely that he'd be interested in doing business, much less sharing a meal, with either of the Metaxas brothers again?

Movement from the corner of his eye caught his attention. He turned to watch a dark head pop up from the stairs, look around wildly, and then emerge altogether.

Well, it looked like he wasn't going to have to say anything at all. The circumstances were about to present themselves in all their beautifully blinding detail.

Ari grinned as Elena came out wearing his shirt again, along with a pair of his white linen pants rolled to her ankles.

Troy glanced up from his laptop, took in Elena, who was on the losing end of a battle to stuff her hair under a Seattle Mariners ball cap, and then returned his attention to his computer again.

Ari silently counted the seconds. Three…two…

"Holy Mother of God!" Troy jumped from his chair so fast he nearly toppled his table, contents and all, straight over the side of the deck.

Not that it mattered. He wasn't going to need any of the items anymore, anyway.

Elena made a beeline for Ari, her face looking a little too blanched for his liking. "I need to get back to the villa," she whispered harshly. "Can you arrange for a skiff?"

"Ari! I need to speak to you. Now!" Troy said.

He held up his hand to his brother, his attention fully on the woman who looked like she was about to jump out of her skin. "I just ordered breakfast for us."

Pain loomed large in her dark eyes.

"Ari!"

"I can't," Elena whispered. "I just can't…"

Troy crossed the deck, moving toward him. Ari turned on him. "Can't you see I'm busy right now, Troy? I'll be with you in a minute."

Elena started walking away, but Ari grasped her arm.

"What in the hell are you doing?" Troy demanded, refusing to wait.

Ari had one person trying to get away from him, and he couldn't get rid of another. Talk about being between a rock and a stubborn place.

"I need to get a skiff back to the island," Elena said pleadingly. "It's too late to hope that no one's noticed me missing, but maybe it's not too late to salvage everything…"

She trailed off, apparently seeing something on Ari's face that stopped her from continuing.

Troy finally released his grip and began walking away.

"Damn it, now, where are you going?" Ari asked.

"To get the lady a skiff…"

He quickly moved out of earshot and Ari was left staring at Elena, unable to believe what she'd just said.

"You mean…are you saying…" He swallowed hard. She

couldn't possibly be serious? She was going to go ahead with the wedding? After all that had passed between them last night?

His mind filled with the memory of her quiet moans, her arching back, her ardent cries. He'd been so sure she'd felt as moved as he had. He'd never stopped to consider that she might get up this morning and ride straight out of his life as if nothing had happened. It wasn't possible. Didn't she know that everything had changed? That there was no going back from this?

Elena was silent for a long moment, staring down at the bag she held that presumably contained her shoes and dress. When she raised her damp eyes to him, Ari felt like she'd just socked him in the gut.

"I'm sorry," she whispered. "This is something I've got to do."

"No, you don't. Where's it written? Tell me so I can go tear up the contract." He must have tightened his grip on her slender wrist because she winced. He forced himself to let her go, cursing himself for his overbearing behavior.

But, damn it, he didn't want to let her off this boat. Ever. He wanted to sweep her up into his arms and carry her back down the stairs and never let her out of his bed.

"Things change," he said, sounding weak even to his own ears. "You can't tell me that last night…meant nothing to you."

She looked away again. "Last night was last night, Ari." She searched his eyes as if begging him to understand. "And today is today."

"Today you get married."

Troy returned to the stern and Ari made out the sound of a motor starting up as the skiff that had been secured to the side of the boat was manned.

"All set," his brother said, grasping Elena's other arm. "Follow me, then, and we'll get you on your way."

Elena reluctantly let Troy lead her to the ladder as the skiff pulled up next to it.

"Elena," Ari said so silently he nearly didn't hear the word himself.

"I'm sorry," she said as Troy took the bag from her hand and tossed it to the skiff. "I'm so very sorry…"

8

"WHAT IN THE HELL were you thinking? Or, maybe the correct question is, what in the hell body part were you thinking with?" Troy asked, facing off with Ari after they'd watched the skiff cut the water, back to the island. "Jesus, Ari, you slept with the bride of the man we're looking to help us save our town. How could you even consider it?"

Ari moved to turn away, so filled with pent up energy that he was half afraid he might hit his brother for aiding Elena in her escape. If only he had a few more minutes to talk to her. To kiss her. To make her remember last night…

"Oh, no. I'm not letting you off the hook this time, little brother," Troy said.

"When have you ever let me off easy on anything?"

"What? When? Oh, I know. Whenever we travel somewhere on business and you disappear to go out and have a little fun. When you act like there's not a damn thing wrong, that Dad's not ill, and that the company's not facing bankruptcy without this deal with Philippidis? At every turn, off you go, acting like the American playboy who has access to limitless resources, bedding any woman who'll have you."

Ari stared at him.

Troy sighed and paced a short ways away. "You could have screwed anyone on the entire island. Why did it have to be her?"

"I didn't screw her," he growled.

Troy looked a breath away from hitting him. Which would be all right with Ari, because he could use a good excuse to hit something himself. More specifically, he'd like to knock that know-it-all expression from his brother's face.

"Oh, no. You didn't screw her. The two of you experienced love at first sight." He pointed toward the island. "That's why she hightailed it off the boat to return to the man she should be marrying. Because you rocked her world and she decided that, gee, she couldn't marry one of the richest men in the world. She wanted one of the poorest."

Ari advanced on him and Troy backed up. "Are you calling her a whore?"

"Her? No. I'm not saying anything about her. I'm questioning the constitution of your own moral integrity."

"So you're calling me the whore."

"If the condom fits." Troy stalked back to the table, then picked up the contracts there and threw them at him. "Damn it, Ari, how could you have done this?"

"Funny, the question that comes to the forefront of my mind is how could I not have." He grabbed the contracts and slapped them against his chest. "You're right. I've been with a lot of women in my life. But Elena…she's different, somehow. Special…"

"Yes, because she's off limits."

"No, because I was drawn to her before I even knew who she was. We met in the market yesterday morning, long before dinner last night."

Troy appeared not to believe him.

"Fine. Don't buy it. Frankly, I don't give a shit." He pointed at him. "But I'll tell you what. I don't intend to let things go so easily. I'm going after her."

"Oh, no, you're not. If you value anything in this life, Ari, I beg you to stay on board this boat until we leave."

Ari stiffened.

"If luck is on our side, she can convince everyone that nothing happened."

"No, if luck is on your side," Ari corrected.

"No, Ari. I meant 'our.' As in Dad's side, the company's side. The town's side. Right now I could care less about whose side you're on. No. Wait. I know. You're on your own side. Like you always are."

"That's unfair."

"Is it? Because right now, I don't think it is."

Troy closed his laptop, then grabbed the contracts and stuffed them into his bag.

"I'm going downstairs to finish these up. I'm going to try to salvage what I've worked for the past ten months and pray that Philippidis has no idea that you took his wife-to-be on a trial honeymoon. You can decide what you're going to do."

Ari stood, torn. He looked toward shore and Elena, then back to where Troy disappeared belowdecks.

He shouted a curse to the gods above, damning them for getting him into this mess.

And wondering just how in the hell he was supposed to forget a woman who'd moved him as no other ever had…

OKAY, WHO MADE OFF with the old Elena and just where did she go to find her again?

Elena stood under the punishing shower spray, listening to her mother pounding on the locked bathroom door. She wasn't surprised when she'd returned to the villa to find Ekaterina pacing the floor demanding to know her whereabouts from the amused maid. Her mother had advanced on her, throwing questions like stones, each hitting their mark unerringly as her armor wore away with every blow. Elena had fought to focus on the maid who stood in front of the bathroom holding a towel, indicating escape. And Elena had done exactly that, ducking into the other room before she ended up an emotionally bloodied pulp on the chic villa's marble-tiled floor.

For a long time, she'd merely stood leaning against the sink, her chin to her chest, her eyes closed, as she tried to stop the world from spinning. Not even her mother's periodic knocking and demands for answers could compete with her own sense of bewilderment.

Until, finally, her mother had said, "You don't deserve Manolis."

It was then that Elena's head snapped up and she stared at herself in the mirror.

"No, I don't," she'd whispered.

Then she'd finally stripped out of the borrowed clothes, carefully folding them and stashing them for safekeeping before climbing into a shower built for two.

Was it possible that in the darkness of last night, she had so easily forgotten everything else around her? Had she really allowed herself to focus only on what was in her line of sight? Granted permission to her body to do its will?

Ari…

She remembered his hold on her arm…the surprised expression on his face this morning. She swallowed hard.

But the instant she'd woken up to the sunshine slicing across her face, she'd understood that the secrets created in the shadows had been chased away by dawn's bright, unforgiving light.

At least she'd finally found a way to warm her cold feet.

Elena groaned.

No matter how hard she tried, she couldn't seem to oust last night's images from her mind. The hot waters sluicing over her naked body reminded her of Ari's hands sliding over her, knowing and attentive, creating need and slaking it simultaneously. She squeezed her thighs together only to remember how he'd put his mouth there, laving her until she reached a pleasure point no other man had been capable of achieving. Water dropped from the tips of her breasts and through the shallow crevice between her legs, calling to mind how he'd filled her so utterly, so completely, touching places she hadn't known existed, introducing her to her own body and the magnificent joys it could produce.

How had she gone so long without knowing the magic of sex? Of multiple orgasms? Of finding and residing in a place so outside of herself as to be surreal?

More importantly, how did she proceed in the path she predetermined for herself knowing these new truths?

Out there somewhere, over a hundred and fifty guests prepared to attend the lavish wedding ceremony. Manolis would still be on his yacht, coming in for the luncheon planned for the rest of the guests that she wouldn't attend, since it was bad luck for the groom to see his bride before they met in front of the church.

Of course, it didn't bode well that the bride had enjoyed the attentions of another man the night before the ceremony, either.

The shower spray began to turn cold. She shivered and shut it off, standing for a long moment before reaching for a towel. Where just a short time ago, she'd known exactly where her life was heading and with whom, now she stared at a gaping void filled with shocking question marks, each one larger and more insistent than the one before.

Her mother pounded on the door again, letting her know

that the world wasn't about to stand still while she figured everything out. "Elena! Damn it, girl, open the door this minute. The hairdresser's here."

She slowly reached for a towel and wiped the dampness from her face, biting down on the clean cotton as tears filled her eyes…

ARI JUMPED FROM the skiff before it had properly docked, nearly landing in the sea. The near miss barely registered as he ran up the steep walkway to the top of the cliffs.

He'd spent twenty minutes on the boat driving himself insane with an incessant series of what-ifs before grabbing a shower and deciding that he couldn't act as if nothing had happened. The business contract and his brother be damned, he wanted— no, *needed*—Elena in his life. He would *not* stand by and watch her marry another man. As crazy as it all sounded, he needed to find out if what happened between them was a one-time, one-night deal, or if it was the beginning of something even greater.

Okay, so maybe he had earned a reputation as being a man of little ambition. But he seemed to be the only one who knew that was because Troy worried and worked enough for both of them. Any attempts on Ari's behalf to play a role were always firmly rebuffed.

But when all was said and done, he was ready to step in at a moment's notice. And when he wanted something, he went after it full throttle.

And he wanted Elena.

Whether or not he could get her was another matter. But he had to try. He couldn't let things stand between them as they had on the sailboat, with her in a state of panic, and his brother expediting her exit. He had no idea what he'd say to her once he had her ear, but his argument would probably be similar to the one he gave last night. His urgings would be even more urgent now, considering that in a few short hours she would become someone else's wife.

Did he want to marry her?

The question caught him up short and his pace slowed even as sweat coated his forehead. It was too soon to even consider it, but...

His brother's words flashed through his mind. Was he really capable of throwing away ten months of hard work and the future of Earnest, Washington, because of his unknown feelings for this one woman?

Yes, he realized, he was. While he might not know if she was the woman he would marry, he did know that the thought of sleeping in his bed without her in it was driving him mad. And, the thought of her sleeping with another man made him madder still.

He quickened his pace, immune to the beauty of the island that had captivated him only the day before. He'd found an even greater beauty in Elena.

Ten minutes later he wound his way around to the villas where she was staying, preparing himself for what was to come. She had hurried from the sailboat so quickly, they hadn't had an opportunity to talk.

Would she talk to him now?

By damn, he would make her. Just as he had last night.

Of course, he couldn't exactly dump her into the Aegean now, but surely even she understood that things had changed. Neither of them were the same people they'd been even twelve hours ago. At the very least, he had to convince her not to marry Philippidis.

He recalled his brother's insinuations that Elena was marrying for money, and his instant defense of her.

Could he truly say that she wasn't marrying for those reasons? No. But he sensed that she wasn't. He'd bet his bottom dollar that a woman willing to sacrifice her future for marriage to a man twice her age wouldn't have responded to him so openly as she had, so innocently. She wouldn't have appeared so touchingly lost this morning, as if she'd known everything had changed.

Unfortunately, it looked as if he was going to have to bet that bottom dollar to find out.

Ari drew to a halt, staring at the white, arched doorway that led to the exclusive villas. He wasn't surprised to see Philippidis's goon standing there, his hand behind his back, guarding the entrance.

No, he was surprised. But he was disappointed. It meant that his job had just become that much more difficult...and critical. Because it seemed that it was full steam ahead for today's nuptials...

9

ELENA HEARD THE RUCKUS outside the villa but was forced to remain seated in front of the vanity, while the hairdresser fussed over her. In the mirror, she watched as her mother went to the patio door, then nearly ripped the curtains from the rods as she drew them closed.

"What is it?" Elena asked, trying to get up.

The hairdresser stopped her with a hand to her shoulder, telling her Elena would ruin all her work if she moved.

"Screw my hair," she said, rising anyway.

Her mother stepped in front of her to stop her progress. "Sit down, Elena."

"Get out of my way, Mother."

Ekaterina blinked at her. Never had Elena spoken to her in such an impertinent manner. Nor had she ever called her Mother. It was always Mama or Mom, but never Mother.

"Elena, you need to ask yourself an important question before you do this—is it really worth risking a wonderful future with a wonderful man?"

Elena attempted to pass her.

"Do you really want to hurt Manolis?"

That did give her pause.

Of course she didn't want to hurt him. He'd been so good to her and her family. A gentleman through and through. The last thing she wanted was to cause him any pain.

The crash of something sent them both rushing to the patio.

Elena pushed aside the curtains and opened the door, then stood looking at where Manolis's bodyguard stood over Ari, who was sprawled on top of a broken clay pot of hydrangeas.

Gregoris appeared to be reaching for something under his white jacket. Something Elena feared might be a gun.

She placed herself between him and Ari, who was rubbing his jaw and stumbling to his feet.

"What are you doing here?" she demanded of the overgrown Greek.

Then it hit her.

Manolis knew.

Elena's throat closed off, refusing air as she considered her circumstances. If Gregoris had been sent to guard her, and was fighting to keep Ari from reaching her, then Manolis knew about last night. He knew she had spent the night with another man.

Why else would the bodyguard be stationed there? He'd never been anywhere near her villa as far as she knew.

Until now.

Ari charged the larger man and Elena winced as his fist met with the other man's jaw, sending him stumbling backward.

"That's for hitting me," Ari said.

Gregoris regained his balance and withdrew the gun he'd been reaching for.

"Stop it!"

Elena had thought she'd issued the command. Instead, it had been her mother.

She watched in amazement as Ekaterina crossed the patio and smacked the angry Greek across the face with a loud crack. "What in the hell do you think you're doing? I want you out of here. Now!" she commanded.

Gregoris blinked at her a couple of times and put the gun

away. Then his gaze landed on Ari again. He extended a finger in his direction and waggled it, as if to say he'd see him later. Then he stalked from the courtyard, likely on his way to report to his boss.

But Elena couldn't concern herself with that right now.

"Jesus," she said, turning to inspect the damage to Ari's face.

Her heart pitched. Was it even remotely possible that she'd forgotten how strikingly handsome he was? Especially when he was looking at her as if the sun set and rose over her?

"Elena," he breathed, as if he'd been holding her name in for a long time and was glad to finally say it.

"What are you doing?" she asked, her mind beginning to settle. "He could have killed you."

"And I him."

Ridiculously, a giggle bubbled up from her chest. She never giggled.

A grin turned up the corners of his mouth and she swallowed hard, filled with the sudden desire to kiss him.

Kiss him.

Right there in front of her mother and God and everyone. On her wedding day.

"What are you doing here?" she whispered.

His expression reflected surprise, as if she should know what he was doing and exactly what he wanted.

"I can't let you get married," he said simply, as if his words made all the sense in the world.

THERE. HIS CARDS were on the table. Again.

Uh-oh. He didn't like the look in her eyes. He also didn't like that she appeared knee deep in wedding preparation, her hair half done up, a string of pearls around her neck.

"You can't possibly intend to go through with it?" he asked.

Her mother chose that moment to remind them of her presence. If he'd been hoping her standing up to Manolis's goon meant he was in her good graces, he was proven wrong.

"Of course she's going through with it. Manolis Philippidis is a good man who can provide for my daughter." She gave him a once-over that made it clear she found him lacking. "What do you have to give her? Besides a lot of heartache."

"Mama," Elena said quietly.

But the elder Anastasios wasn't done. "You know he'll be back, don't you? Probably with reinforcements." She turned toward her daughter. "Which means Manolis will know, if he doesn't already. In fact, I'm afraid he may already know anyway."

"What is there to know, Mama?"

"That you spent the night with this man."

Ari set his jaw.

"That's right. I know. I may not have known it was him until just now, but when I returned to the villas last night and discovered you weren't in your room, I knew that something must have happened. And now I know what."

"You don't have any idea what happened."

"Don't I?" She arched a high brow. "I am a woman, same as you, Elena. I know how a woman feels. And when you two met last night, I knew it had not been your first time. More than that, I knew what you shared was not casual."

She shook her head. "This isn't like you, Elena. Think this through, I beg of you. You've always been a practical girl." She looked at Ari again. "This is only about sex. That will fade. And then what will you be left with? With Manolis, there is love."

Ari watched Elena's beautiful face fall as her mother spoke. His own mother had died when he was young, so he didn't have much personal experience with maternal power. But he got the very distinct impression that Ekaterina Anastasios knew exactly what to say to her daughter to manipulate her in a certain direction. She'd been doing it since birth.

What chance did he stand against that?

"Mama, can you please leave us alone for a minute?" Elena asked.

She was going to ask him to leave. To allow her the freedom to marry Philippidis. He could see it in her every movement.

And, apparently, so could her mother. Because rather than argue, she nodded and went back into the villa.

Ari paced back and forth, reaching, grabbing for an argument that could not only counter Ekaterina's, but beat it flat out before Elena had a chance to refuse him.

"You had cold feet," he said.

Her gaze jerked up from where she'd been staring at the destroyed clay pot.

"That's what your mother told you last night."

She sighed. "We already discussed this…"

"Yes, but have you truly explored all the possible reasons why?" He was losing her, he could tell. Hell, he was flattering himself to think he'd ever had her to begin with. "Your mother said that there is love with…him." He couldn't bring himself to say Philippidis's name. "Do you love him?"

"You have no right to ask me that."

"Don't I?"

He was losing ground fast. He wasn't going to win her over by questioning her intentions.

He held up his hands. "Okay, we'll forget that for now." He drew a deep breath. "But can I ask if he loves you?"

Her eyes narrowed.

"What I mean is, does he love you the way you deserve to

be loved? With the fever and passion of youth? Or with the cold, doting detachment of an older man? Do you want him to be the father of your children? Will he be able to get out on a soccer field with them, play with them? Will he even be around when they graduate high school?"

"That's not fair."

"Isn't it? I don't think it's fair that I'm being shown the door because what I offer isn't significant enough. Maybe you need a better, fuller, more balanced picture here before you make your decision."

She tilted her head. "Are you saying you want to be the father of my children?"

Ari blinked at her.

She looked disappointed in his lack of response.

"What do you want me to say, Elena? Do you want me to proclaim my undying love for you and beg you to be the mother of my children? Would you even believe me if I did?" He shook his head. "I'm not going to lie to you and say that I know this, what's ignited between us, is forever."

She appeared to be about to turn away from him. And he was terrified it would be forever.

"But I'm convinced enough that this—what we have— very well might be that forever, ten children kind of love. I wouldn't be standing here, putting everything on the line, if I didn't think so."

She was quiet for a long time. But at least she was listening.

He heard her thick swallow. Then she whispered, "How do I know that you're not playing a game? That I'm some sort of emotional, macho trophy to be hung on your wall once everything is said and done?"

"Is that what you think?" His voice was almost as low as hers was.

No. That's not what she thought. But, like he'd suggested, she was considering all the angles.

"You admitted yourself that you've been with a lot of women, Ari. What makes you so convinced that I might be the one? Because I'm about to marry someone else?"

"No," he said, shaking his head. "This has nothing to do with you. It has to do with me. What I feel when I'm with you…it's unlike anything I've experienced before. And it began before I knew you were about to marry him."

She couldn't accuse him of lying there. Their alleyway makeout session had been as out of character for him as he'd suspected was for her.

"So, I guess in a way, you could say that I'm doing this for my own selfish reasons." He stepped closer to her. "Not because you're some trophy to be won. But because, damn it, I can't get enough of you. I want you in my bed. In my life. And the thought of you not being there…makes me want to hit something."

Ari had never felt so vulnerable, so laid bare before someone else. He didn't know whether he should throw her over his shoulder and kidnap her, this time for real, or if he should run away as far as he could, as fast as he could.

He heard the patio door open and knew his time had run out. Her mother had given him all the opportunity she was going to. Perhaps, even as he'd realized she'd won Elena over earlier, she could see that he was also having an impact on her.

"Elena," she said quietly.

Ari's every muscle seemed to vibrate as he waited for her to choose. "Please," he said. "Don't marry him. You have to be wondering if you ever would have slept with me if, indeed, you were destined to marry another man."

He'd hurt her. He witnessed the cloud of pain in her eyes and wanted to immediately brush it away.

"That, more than anything, should be enough to convince you that he isn't the man for you."

"And you think you are."

He held her gaze for a long moment. "I don't know, Elena. But I would like the chance to find out."

"Elena," her mother said again.

Ari desperately hoped that she was going to come to him.

Instead, she looked down at the broken pot again and said, "I've...got to go."

10

SHE LOOKED LIKE A PRINCESS.

She felt like a frog.

"You're beautiful," Aphrodite said from behind Elena. "Any man would be honored to call you wife."

"I wouldn't be too sure about that," she murmured.

Elena caught herself absently plucking at the Swarovski crystals hand sewn into the fitted, sweetheart-cut bodice of the wedding dress. Vera Wang. What bride didn't dream of getting married in a handmade Vera Wang gown?

Unfortunately, Elena's dream was proving to be a nightmare.

The past three hours had passed in a blur. A light lunch had been served, but she couldn't remember eating anything. Bridesmaids had come and gone, cooing over their dresses, her dress and the beauty of the occasion. Her mother had hovered constantly nearby, as if afraid Elena might bolt. And Elena had been fluffed, powdered and waxed, amazed when the makeup artist had worked on even her bare shoulders and arms, clucking when Elena protested as she pointed out that the bride should look perfect on her wedding day.

Elena wanted to shout that she wasn't perfect.

But she hadn't. She'd merely moved through the hours in a daze, trying to hold on to a single thought, come to some sort of decision about everything before she found the decision made for her.

Aphrodite smoothed the train and then straightened to meet her gaze in the mirror. Her intense expression made a shiver travel down Elena's spine. "I am positive that any man would be honored to call you his wife."

She got the very distinct impression that the plucky maid wasn't talking about her intended.

Elena's mother walked back into the room, looking fantastic in her own designer mother-of-the-bride gown. Then Elena's brother stepped up beside her, and she smiled at him in his custom tux. Given that her late father couldn't give her away, her brother had accepted the role when Elena had asked.

Her family…

A wet knot lodged in her throat as she looked at the two of them. They were the only constants in her life. And they were both so damned happy that she was marrying Manolis that she wanted to cry for them.

"The car is waiting," her mother said.

Okay. This was it.

Elena slowly walked toward the door. Everything was arranged. The *stefana*—bridal crowns—had been delivered to the spectacular blue-domed Greek Orthodox cathedral, along with the rings. The reception was all set up and ready to go on the sweeping patio on a rocky outcropping overlooking the deep blue Aegean Sea.

This was supposed to be the first day of the rest of her life.

Why did she feel like it was her last?

She censored herself. It wasn't fair to Manolis to think that way. He'd never strong-armed her into anything, unlike Ari, who had essentially kidnapped her last night. He'd treated her with the utmost respect and, yes, love; nothing less.

Guilt swirled with regret in her stomach until she was afraid she'd be sick.

Her mother seemed to sense her hesitation and took her arm, guiding her toward the door. "What a lovely bride you make, *agape mou*. You make me proud."

When they emerged into the bright sunlight, Elena wavered, then was buoyed on by her brother offering his arm.

Why did she suddenly get the feeling the three of them were marrying Manolis Philippidis?

"WHERE DO YOU THINK you're going?" Troy demanded when Ari emerged onto the deck after changing into appropriate bride-stealing attire.

"What are you doing here? I thought you were going to stay in town after lunch so you could attend the wedding?"

Troy got up from where he'd been working on his laptop. "Manolis refused to sign the papers until after the wedding," he said. "And I got the very distinct impression that neither of us is still invited."

"At least he didn't say that he wouldn't sign them."

"He won't if this wedding doesn't go through."

Ari's footsteps slowed as he walked toward the ladder.

"I swear, if you don't turn around now, Ari…"

"What?" he asked. "You'll kick my ass? Throw me in the Aegean?" He shook his head without turning to look at his brother. "Trust me, Troy, nothing you could dream up can come close to matching the thought of her marrying that man."

"Don't you think you've done enough to stop her already?"

Ari closed his eyes and drew a deep breath, trying to ignore the way the words stung.

"I mean, if she's still planning to marry the guy after everything you've done, then it's my guess that, well, she really wants to marry him."

The stinging ate at him until it created a gaping wound Troy seemed intent on rubbing salt into.

Troy came to stand next to him and together they stared out at the great expanse of sea before them. "I know that you thought this woman was the one for you. Or at least you convinced yourself that she might be. But when is enough enough, Ari? When you've destroyed everything and everyone around you?"

"I'm not intentionally hurting anyone."

"Aren't you? I say that if you go to that island now…well, you'll be doing exactly that." He felt Troy's hand on his shoulder. "Including hurting yourself."

EVERYTHING WAS absolutely perfect. Exactly as it should be on a woman's wedding day. Wispy white clouds meandered above, the sun was shining, and the blue-domed church emerged a piece of colorful art against the backdrop of sea and sky.

"Are you ready?" her brother asked.

Elena hadn't realized the car had stopped at the church steps until he spoke.

No! she wanted to shout. She was nowhere near ready. She didn't even know if she wanted to go through with this, much less do it today.

Then she spotted her groom standing in front of the church doors, beaming at her, and she knew a bit of relief.

If there was one thing she'd always been able to do with Manolis, it was talk. He'd listen patiently to her for hours on end as she'd spoken about the grief associated with the death of her father, a passing that had resulted in the death of a way of life for the entire family once they'd discovered the restaurant was in more debt than they could ever hope to repay and that he had no insurance. Funeral costs alone had been an incredible burden, and there had been no way that they could grant her father's wishes that he be buried alongside his family in Greece. Instead, they'd been forced to have him cremated, and only now had they traveled to Kalamata in the Peloponnese to scatter his ashes at the cemetery where eight generations of Anastasioses had been laid to rest, waiting for his return.

It was Manolis who had stepped in as her father's oldest friend and helped them through. He'd reached out a hand that they hesitantly took.

And it was Manolis who she had slowly come to love. She'd believed that he'd make a great father. A marvelous husband.

And then came Ari…

Elena ousted him from her mind. He had no place being there.

Alex climbed from the other side of the car and came around to open her door. She hadn't realized that guests stood off to the sides in their wedding best until they applauded the appearance of the bride. She took Alex's extended hand and climbed out of the car as gracefully as she could in the meringue-type concoction that floated around her legs. As she stood, facing her groom from across the strategically painted square that separated them, she knew a bit of calm. The same calm she'd felt when he'd first proposed to her three months ago. This was a man who would protect her. He'd make sure she and her family never wanted for anything.

"Are you sure you aren't replacing your late father with a new one?" Words Ari had spoken during their night together came back to haunt her. *"Gratitude isn't love, Elena."*

She fastened a smile on her face. Yes, it was, she silently

answered. Just because she was grateful for all Manolis had done, it was the friendship she shared with him that made her think what they shared could stretch far into the future.

"What about sex?"

Sex was fleeting, she told herself. It took what she and Manolis had to make a marriage last. Like what her mother and father had.

Alex offered his arm and she looked into his handsome face. She placed her hand on her brother's forearm and slowly began making her way toward her groom.

This was going to work. Last night was a mere blip on the radar. Temporary insanity. Something she would forget. Ari was a fun one-night stand; Manolis was forever.

They grew nearer and her resolve grew stronger.

Until she was near enough to look into Manolis's eyes.

Her heart skipped a beat at the unfamiliar glint that resided in the brown-green depths. His mouth might be smiling, but it was a mask. Inside he was angry. *Very* angry.

Elena blinked. She'd never seen him lose his temper. No matter the infraction. He was always easygoing and patient. This glimpse of a different Manolis sent a tremor of uneasiness snaking down her spine.

Alex stepped forward. "I and my family are honored to offer you our sister and daughter," he said, taking her hand and extending it toward Manolis.

His skin was cold.

That's the first thing Elena registered.

His grip was too tight.

That was the second.

And for the first time since she'd met him, she knew fear.

"Manolis?" she whispered.

He knew. She'd suspected as much earlier when his bodyguard had been stationed outside her villa. He knew and he wasn't happy about it. More than that, she was afraid she saw sheer hatred simmering there in his gaze.

Why, then, was he going through with this? Why did he still want to marry her?

That morning she'd accused Ari of pursuing her as some sort of sick game. He wanted her because everyone told him he couldn't have her. He wanted her because she was set to marry someone else. Not merely just any somebody, but a very powerful one. Surely that would have landed him a special clout in certain circles, even if it also meant that he wouldn't be getting the contract he and his brother were seeking.

But as she looked at Manolis now, she wondered if she'd hurt him beyond any apology. And that he was going ahead with the wedding merely to prove that he could. To show the man who had challenged his standing that *he* was the one in power. The one who had control.

Manolis tucked Elena's hand into his arm and began to open the door to the church.

Elena dug in her heels.

"Manolis, wait," she whispered.

Her heart beat a dull rhythm in her chest. She was aware of every eye on them both inside and outside the church.

He didn't deserve this, her mind whispered. She'd betrayed him. She was to blame for the way he was looking at her. It was up to her to make it up to him. And she'd have years to do exactly that.

But what about you? her heart whispered. Was this any way to begin a lifelong union together? Built on such pain? Such anger? Such false pride?

And suddenly, she understood that she couldn't go ahead with this.

"Elena, come," Manolis said between clenched teeth.

She stared at him for a long moment, and then she shook her head. "We need to talk."

He tugged on her hand. "There will be plenty of time for that later."

"No, Manolis. We need to talk now."

He didn't budge, merely stared at her, his anger no longer hidden.

"It's up to you," she murmured. "Either we quietly go around to the courtyard together now, smiling, where we can talk. Or I leave." When his eyes narrowed to dangerous slits, she added, "You decide."

"What is there to talk about, Elena?" he asked, and shrugged as if there was no problem, but even that movement looked stiff and angry. "You betrayed me with another man. I am man enough to accept that. I forgive you. Now come on, let's get married."

She squinted at him, trying to reconcile the man in front of her with the man she'd once agreed to marry. "I haven't asked for your forgiveness," she said quietly.

The instant the words were out of her mouth, she realized she'd said them in order to provoke a reaction.

And it came in the form of a hard slap across her face.

HE WAS TOO LATE.

The words echoed through Ari's head as he raced the rented Audi convertible toward the cathedral where the unblessed event was scheduled to take place. He ground the gears as he shifted the manual transmission a little too quickly, his foot a shade off with the clutch.

Cars were restricted from a good deal of the island, but since the Philippidis wedding was a large affair, it was being held at a church a little ways away from the cliff dwellings, allowing automobile access and traffic.

He spotted the bride's car parked in front of the church and his heart nearly stopped in his chest.

God, no...

He squealed to a stop in front of the black Mercedes and half leapt from the car without opening the door. Only then did he notice that Elena hadn't yet entered the church. Instead, she was standing outside, facing Manolis Philippidis. She held a hand to her cheek, said something to her groom, and then turned and began running toward the car.

Ari's gaze went back to Manolis, just now seeing that the older man was enraged. And he was now focusing that emotion full force in Ari's direction.

"Elena!" he called, rushing to her.

She stopped in front of him and looked up, her eyes bright with tears, her cheek red.

"Come on," he said, motioning toward his rental.

She didn't say anything for a long moment and appeared to be having difficulty catching her breath. She took in where his car blocked in the Mercedes.

"I don't want anything to do with either one of you," she whispered, and then turned in the opposite direction and began running.

Ari stood watching helplessly as the beautiful vision in white moved farther away from him. He didn't know if her veil had come loose or if she had removed it, but it floated in the air, hovering there long after she was gone.

11

THE REALITIES OF Elena's wedding day actions manifested themselves in a number of ways. Not the least of which was her family's quality of life.

Had they really become so dependent on Manolis so fast? After they'd closed the restaurant, her brother had gone to work for Manolis's Pacific NW headquarters in Seattle. A job he'd lost due to "personnel cutbacks" within a week of their return from Greece. The note for the outstanding balance of the mortgage on her parents' house had been called due, payment demanded in full within ninety days because Manolis had cosigned for a refinance deal with a better interest rate. And, unbeknownst to Elena, her mother had been receiving a weekly check from the billionaire, whose only interest, he'd said, was to see his best friend's widow get back on her feet after such a terrible blow. It was a check that no longer arrived.

With her brother forced to move back home after his job loss, Elena had to face not only her mother's scowl every morning, but Alex's as well.

"Maybe it's not too late to patch things up," her mother had repeated so often Elena heard it in her sleep.

"You should have married him," was Alex's favorite refrain.

On several occasions, she'd considered moving out on her own. But their mounting problems had to be faced as a family. She couldn't abandon her mother. And her brother had never been much of a leader.

So every morning she got up before sunrise, showered, and made sure her brother was out of bed ready to hit the bricks in search of another job, something to replace the low-wage telemarketer position he'd had for the past three weeks. And she went to the restaurant that had stood boarded up for the past year. The only saving grace was that they still owned the land and the building—Manolis had somehow overlooked taking away that one anchor.

She hated viewing events in that unflattering light, but after all that had transpired since she'd stood before him at the church, she'd been shocked by her former fiancé's vicious acts of revenge.

Never would she have believed him capable of this type of behavior.

With her mother's grudging help—even as Ekaterina tried everything she could to try to convince Elena to seek Manolis's forgiveness—she opened the restaurant back up, starting with breakfast, which offered the greatest rate of return even with the specials she came up with to tempt customers back.

She consulted with her friend Merianna, who was a damn good attorney, to find out whether or not Manolis would be able to recoup the monies he'd given them to cover her father's bad business debts. This time, she wanted to be ahead in the game instead of offering herself up so willingly as victim.

Most days she also worked as a waitress at a restaurant across town where the hours were long but the tips were good. Anything to put enough money together to save her mother's house.

If every now and again her thoughts turned to Ari, she didn't readily admit it to anyone but herself. She'd read a newspaper piece on his brother and the family company a week or so ago that covered the Philippidis deal falling through. While the family wasn't in any way tycoon material, she'd read that they were very well off and already had backup plans in motion to help save the old mill town about an hour south of Seattle.

Elena had allowed herself a few moments of relief that Manolis hadn't been able to hurt Ari. And then hid the paper from her mother in case Ekaterina got it in her head that she should marry someone else for money.

The way Elena saw it, life had been challenging before. It was now challenging again. She didn't care about the money. So long as you worked hard and had a plan, she strongly believed there wasn't anything you couldn't do.

If only she could convince her mother of the same.

"You should sell the jewelry," Ekaterina said that morning as she buttered toast at the restaurant.

Elena checked hash browns and flipped pancakes. "I've already told you that I'm sending it all back, Mama. I don't want you to mention it again."

"Then why haven't you sent it yet?"

That was the question, wasn't it?

Back at the house, she had a large box stuffed full of all the designer clothes, shoes and handbags Manolis had bought for her either directly or indirectly. Nestled on top was a box with the jewelry he'd given her, including the ten-carat diamond engagement ring that was worth a small fortune.

She wasn't sure why she hadn't sent the items back yet. Perhaps she was waiting for him to ask for them. In fact, she was surprised he hadn't done so yet. The thought of slipping a box that held so many valuable items into the mail was unsettling. And she certainly couldn't afford the postage insurance to cover it.

She'd considered calling his secretary and arranging to have someone come pick the box up. But every time she thought about it, Manolis did something else to make her rethink the matter.

She and her mother plated the two breakfast special orders of pancakes, two eggs, hash browns and toast and her mother slid around the counter to serve them to a couple in a corner booth.

The restaurant wasn't quite up to its former glory, but it had passed a health inspection last week and the customers they attracted didn't seem to mind that half the dining area was cordoned off for simplicity's sake, or that the one waitress, her mother, was a little on the slow side.

"More coffee?" she heard her mother ask.

Elena stood in the open window cut into the wall between the dining area and kitchen and watched her.

Ekaterina seemed to have aged ten years in the month since their return. Elena's stomach ached, knowing she was to blame. She glanced at a picture on the wall above the framed first dollar her father had made at the restaurant over thirty years ago. The photo was of the four of them, taken a long time ago. They'd never had a lot of money, but they'd always been happy together. Their smiles told of that, as did Elena's memories.

They'd be happy again.

"You just sighed again," her mother told her as she came back with another order from a table of three that had come in.

"I did not."

"Yes, you did. You sigh more than you talk these days. I think you miss Manolis."

Elena smiled wryly. "Fat chance." She broke a couple of eggs into a bowl and then poured them into a hot pan. She picked up a spatula and then dropped it back to the prep counter, causing a clatter. "You know, life would be a lot easier if you'd stop hounding me about Manolis. I will not call him. Ever. The sooner you accept that, the better off we'll all be."

"Better off?" her mother asked. She swept a hand toward the other side of the kitchen that was closed because of a broken oven and water damage in the corner that they had painted over to keep mold from forming, but couldn't afford to repair. "How will we be better off, Elena?"

She came around the counter and checked the eggs.

"I don't understand how you could have turned so quickly," Ekaterina said. "So he slapped you. Even you'll admit, you probably deserved it. No, you did deserve it, for betraying him like that."

It wasn't the first time she'd heard the argument. And it wasn't the first time she'd told her mother, "I can't believe you're still siding with him after all he's done."

"A man like Manolis doesn't get where he is without being strong and a bit ruthless. He's hurt. He's lashing out."

"The only thing that's hurt is his pride." Elena hadn't seen any pain in his gaze when she'd faced him. Only anger.

"And how is that any different?"

"What kind of marriage do you think I'd have if I called him right now? Right this minute?" Elena asked. "If he'd even have me."

"Oh, he'll have you all right," her mother assured her. "It would be the perfect salve to his wounded ego."

"And the first part of my question?"

"You'll suffer. A little bit. But once you're in his bed, he'll forget soon enough."

Elena winced. "What, are you my pimp now?"

Her mother's mouth fell open. "How dare you talk to me like that."

"Well, that's what you are, aren't you? You're suggesting that I beg forgiveness from a man who is trying to put us out of our house, Mama. And that I marry him and…service him to soothe his bruised ego."

"You'd rather we go homeless."

"If that's the only alternative, then, yes, I would."

"Come on, Elena. You're acting like you're the wounded one. You can't tell me you really loved Manolis to begin with."

"What?" She was appalled that her mother was suggesting otherwise.

"Your father left us in dire straits. We needed the money and you came through for your family."

She gasped. "I loved him."

Her mother snorted. "And that's why it was so easy for you to sleep with another man the night before your wedding?"

Elena felt her face go hot.

The eggs were ruined. She picked up the pan and tilted the contents into a nearby garbage bin.

"I loved Manolis," she whispered. "But maybe I wasn't in love with him."

"But you are in love with the other man. That…Ari character."

Elena turned her back on her mother and went about making fresh eggs.

She hadn't known Ari long enough to say that. But meeting him…spending time with him, she'd learned there was an important difference between loving someone and being in love with them. She hadn't been "in love" with Manolis.

In all honesty, she probably hadn't loved him, either. Because judging by his recent actions, she hadn't really known him, despite all the time they'd spent together.

Why the act? she wondered. If her mother was right, and men like Manolis had to be ruthless, why then would he act another way with her?

Then, of course, there was the other important reason why she couldn't return to him. While he might be able to forgive her for momentary insanity, he'd never be able to accept another man's child as his own.

Elena slid her hand down over her still-flat stomach and swallowed hard.

"You better turn those out before you burn them, too." Her mother handed her a plate.

They silently plated the two specials along with an order of oatmeal, and her mother went out to serve.

Elena glanced at the clock on the wall. It was almost ten. That gave her a half hour to get home, get showered and changed and go to serve lunch at someone else's restaurant.

She began cleaning up. While her mother would hold down the fort for however long it took to keep the remaining customers happy, the Closed sign would be turned around to discourage further diners. But by next month, Elena hoped that they would have enough capital to begin offering a limited lunch menu.

She started untying her apron when she heard the cowbell over the front door ring. Since everyone there had just been served, it meant that her mother had yet to turn the Closed sign.

She tied the apron again.

"We're closed," her mother said sternly.

Elena turned quickly, wondering who she could be addressing so stridently in front of paying customers.

"The sign says Open."

Her heart skipped a beat. Though she'd only heard the voice for two short days, she'd recognize it anywhere.

Ari...

She ducked down and scrambled to the end of the row where she couldn't be seen from the window.

What was she going to do?

12

ARI IMAGINED A LOT of different scenarios when he tried to seek out Elena, but this definitely hadn't rated in the top five.

He absently rubbed the back of his neck, nodding his apologies to the restaurant customers who stared openly at him and the older Greek woman trying to shout him back out the door.

"I'm not here to eat," he insisted when she said they were no longer serving.

Although Lord knew he could use a good meal. He'd dropped five pounds in the past month because he kept forgetting to eat. He simply hadn't had any appetite for food. He moved through the days, hoping for the dawning of the one when things would get easier. When he wouldn't think of Elena every damn moment of every damn day and life would return to normal.

Instead, the passage of time merely served to intensify his feelings for her. It wasn't the point that even his brother had said to him the other morning, "Christ, Ari, you're actually starting to look physically ill. And, frankly, you're beginning to make me sick."

Troy had just accepted breakfast from the house cook and watched as Ari leaned back away from his own plate and reached for his coffee instead.

"Okay, I get it. This wasn't merely about sex for you." Troy had cut his French toast with agitated chops. "I'd like to say it makes me feel better about losing that blasted deal with Philippidis, but…well, at least knowing you're suffering helps a little."

"Gee, thanks," Ari had said, pushing his plate away.

"Oh, for God's sake, go find the woman already," his brother had mumbled. "Just looking at you makes me want to cut my own wrists with a dull butter knife."

Ari had stared at him as if he was short one sugar cube. Then Troy had slowly grinned.

"Well, what are you waiting for? You've been going like gangbusters at the office, but here at home it's like you're sleepwalking. Do something already, or else I will."

Ari hadn't moved. Truth was, it hadn't been his brother's objection that had stopped him from seeking Elena out. Something else had. A pain that had developed when she'd run away from him outside the church, and refused to go away.

He'd cleared his throat. "What if she doesn't want me?"

Troy had allowed his silverware to clatter to his plate as he glared at his brother. "Well, you won't know that until you go see her, will you?"

Despite his fears, the lick of hope that had run through Ari's chest had begun a string of events that had led him to this restaurant on the outskirts of Seattle.

His brother had been insufferable over the past month. Plans that had been set into motion had to be stopped, rerouted or scrapped altogether. Government stimulus had dried up without the supplemental resources to sustain it. Tries at making inroads with other investment firms had proven futile. And repeated attempts to contact Philippidis's people had ultimately led to the threat of a lawsuit.

Ari had thrown himself into the act of striving to make up for what had happened. He'd flown all over the country, meeting with various capital investors and banks, each time worse than the one before. No one, it seemed, was interested in helping a washed up, old mill town.

Thankfully, the family was still doing well, managing to maintain the lifestyle their father had worked hard to create, and employing more people than was really necessary for the upkeep of the Metaxas estate in order to give a little back. But whenever they left the large grounds, they were reminded that life wasn't going as well for the rest of the town's inhabitants. And, more than ever, Ari felt personally responsible for their continued struggle.

Had he not fallen for Elena, had he controlled himself and allowed her to marry Philippidis, they would have closed the deal. By now the company would have broken ground on the new solar panel manufacturing facility they planned to build, and begun putting town inhabitants back to work: first, the local construction companies, then unemployed mill workers when they went into production six months later.

Now those plans were on indefinite hold. All due to him. And he had nothing to show for it but countless empty bottles of antacid.

Still, despite all the recent hardships, he couldn't help thinking that none of it compared to the angry Greek woman he now faced.

"I need to talk to her," he said quietly.

"I think you've done enough talking," Ekaterina Anastasios refused to back down. She planted her hands on her hips. "Go on. You're not welcome here."

Ari looked around the restaurant's humble interior. A large screen had been set up to separate the dining area into two distinct sections. Perhaps to hide blemishes, as the place was in dire need of renovations and updating, although it was spotlessly clean. Or to limit the customers to one side for ease in serving. He didn't see any other waitstaff, so perhaps they were running on bare minimum.

It hadn't taken long to track Elena down. Or, rather, research her family. A restaurant in business for a good quarter of a century rarely went without some sort of notice. He'd found several good newspaper reviews and pieces that included photos of what he guessed had been Elena's father before he passed away.

Then he'd come across the engagement announcement.

"Local girl set to marry Greek tycoon" had been the accompanying story headline.

He'd also uncovered that the family house sat on the brink of foreclosure, no thanks to Elena's vengeful ex-fiancé, and that she'd reopened the restaurant for limited service two weeks ago.

He figured that would be the best place to approach her. In a public place.

Now he questioned that logic.

If he was going to be rejected again, did he really want it to be in front of a room full of strangers?

Of course, he'd prefer she did the rejecting and not her mother.

"Elena," he called out, craning his neck to see over the screen, and then the window to the kitchen.

"She doesn't want to see you," Ekaterina insisted, giving him a shove toward the door.

"I'd like to hear that from her lips, if you don't mind." He gently but insistently caught her hands in his to keep her from pushing again. "Elena!"

The customers had stopped all pretense of eating and now sat openly watching him.

"Elena!"

Her name rolled out of his mouth naturally and he thought he noticed the slightest edge of desperation to his voice.

Finally, the kitchen door opened and there stood the woman who had haunted his every waking and sleeping moment for the past month.

Merely glimpsing her made him fear that she would haunt him for the rest of his life…

ELENA HAD RUSHED toward the kitchen door. Anything to halt the escalating confrontation in the dining room. But the instant her gaze crashed with Ari's, she was swept back to that Aegean island that seemed so far away. She could nearly smell the gardenias and taste the salty sea on her lips as she licked them.

Realizing she still wore her apron, she hurried to untie it even as she focused on her mother's reddened face.

"I'll handle this, Mother," she said firmly.

Ekaterina opened her mouth several times to object. Elena handed her the apron and then took Ari's arm and led him outside.

It was a rare Seattle day full of bright sunshine. Elena shivered, unsure if it was due to the weather or Ari's nearness.

Was it possible that his presence affected her even more powerfully now? That without the distraction of her engagement and wedding that he was somehow able to draw her entire essence to him? Or had time and circumstances amplified what they had shared, making him the sun emerging from the clouds after a month of relentless rain? Making her even more vulnerable?

She turned to face him, and she found every last chaotic emotion she felt reflected on his handsome face. Her heart beat an erratic rhythm in her chest.

"You look beautiful," he said quietly, his dark gaze holding hers hostage.

Elena swallowed hard and ran her damp palms along the black slacks she wore. She stopped herself from reaching for the plain green rubber band that held her hair back, but just barely. "No, I don't."

His smile was full and utterly convincing. "Yes, you do."

And, suddenly, she felt that she *was* beautiful. At least in his eyes. And her response was complete and overwhelming.

She'd missed him. Incredible, considering that she'd barely had time to get to know him. Or, rather, she'd missed feeling...special. As if everything she ever needed existed there in his eyes. As if he held her heart in the palm of his hand, and that she trusted him utterly to keep it safe.

Before she could prepare herself, he was kissing her. Hungrily, greedily, crowding her to his body as if they were coming home from a late-night date and the next logical destination was her bedroom.

But they weren't in the privacy of her house, they were out in public, in front of the restaurant. A driver honked his horn as the busy traffic zoomed by on the four-lane highway behind her.

Elena tugged her mouth from his, curiously out of breath as she leaned her nose against his chin.

It was then that she realized that it wasn't the exotic Aegean locale that had inspired her atypical behavior a month ago. No, the emotions expanding within her were due to this one man, and this one man alone.

"I'm sorry," he said quietly. "I really hadn't intended to do that."

She looked up at him through the fringe of her lashes. "Hadn't you?"

His grin was quick. "I'd wanted to. Still…want to."

Elena considered everything that had happened in the past month. It was strange that it all looked different now as she stood in front of Ari. Not so important.

"I…"

She waited. Then prompted him, "You…"

"Damn it all, Elena. I've been going through hell these past weeks. Not being able to see you…touch you…"

The heat in her belly surged upward to her chest.

"I kept thinking it would go away. That what happened in Greece…what happened between us was only a dream from which I'd soon wake up…"

Elena could relate.

"Sex."

She blinked. "Pardon me?"

Ari grinned at her. "I thought it had to be all about the sex. My inability to forget you."

She looked away.

"You have to admit, that night was pretty incredible."

She bit her bottom lip. She woke up sometimes two times a night in a bad way, yearning for him, reaching for him, only to realize he wasn't there. And probably wouldn't be again.

"But this…what I'm feeling, it's not about that."

She searched his face.

"Well, it's not *only* about that."

He paced a short ways away then came back again. "I kept trying to convince myself that it was nothing but a one-night stand. That the sex was so mindblowing because of our circumstances. I mean, we barely knew each other…"

Cars continued to drive by, the world continued to turn, but all Elena saw was him.

"But I've come to understand that…well, the sex was so

incredible because...oh, hell, I'm making a mess out of this..."

Elena reached for his hands. "Go on."

He looked into her eyes as if finding courage there. "You're the one for me, Elena. We were meant for each other. That's why that night was so memorable. Why I can't forget about you."

Her breath lodged in her throat.

He dropped to one knee. "And I don't want to go one more night without you."

Another horn honked.

Elena grabbed his hand and anxiously tried to yank him to a standing position. "What are you doing?"

Ari resisted. "I'm proposing to you, Elena." He looked down and then back up again. "Will you marry me?"

Marry him?

She couldn't have been more surprised had he presented her with two first-class tickets back to Greece.

And he couldn't have made her any happier.

But...

"Are you crazy? I don't even know your middle name. And you don't know mine. We don't know anything about each other."

"Constantina." He said her middle name.

He was serious. He really wanted to marry her.

Then it dawned on her. She'd spent the past year convincing herself she knew Manolis. She'd built her life around what had turned out to be little more than a mirage. She'd convinced herself that the affection she'd felt for him could be coaxed into love.

But when it came to Ari...

Well, when it came to Ari, she was in love. Truly. Madly. Deeply.

"No," she said.

He blinked at her.

"Get up off the sidewalk before my mother comes out here with a broom."

"No?"

He finally rose upon her insistence.

"No."

He looked so crushed that it almost broke her heart.

She reached out and touched the side of his face. "No... not now."

It was his turn to be speechless.

Elena smiled. "I love you, Ari. I know that. But a month ago, I thought I loved someone else. Enough to almost marry him."

"But you won't marry me."

"No. Not now. Maybe not ever." Her smile widened. "Maybe next week."

She tried to work her head around her feelings.

"Look, I don't want to be swept off my feet. I don't want to be rescued. I just want to be loved." She wished away the worried expression from his striking face. "Can you do that for me? Can you love me? Just love me? With no expectations to be met? No promises to keep?"

He didn't answer for a long moment.

She was half afraid that he might give her an ultimatum. Marry him or not. No in between.

Then he slowly grinned.

"That depends."

A condition. She didn't like the sound of that.

She began to withdraw her hands, but he held them tight.

"Not the love part. You already have that, Elena. You always will."

Her heart sprouted golden wings.

"It depends on whether your proposal includes lots more of that phenomenal sex."

The joy that burst within her was unequal to anything she'd ever experienced before. Not as Manolis's bride. Not as her parents' daughter. Not at any other time in her life.

She wrapped her arms around him, aware of every inch of him as she kissed him. "That goes without saying," she whispered.

He returned her kiss hotly, his hands pressing her hard against him. "Then I can wait as long as you want."

How stupid she'd been, she thought as liquid heat flowed through her bloodstream. She'd thought a place and a ceremony and a dress made a fairy tale.

All she'd ever needed was this man…

And they lived sexily ever after…

Fairy tales are fairy tales because of the very fact that they never come easy. Elena and Ari learned the hard way that love, real love, does not always come without sacrifice and difficult choices. And it may arrive at your well-fortified gate while you're busy making other plans.

Love is not something that can be planned or mastered, but instead is a gift from the gods that demands complete and utter surrender. Oh, you may choose to ignore it, deny it and pretend it doesn't exist because the timing isn't right, or others stand against it, but the punishment exacted by those same gods will be everlasting. But no matter what promises you might break, or empires may crumble, if you're brave enough to open yourself to that once-in-a-lifetime love, then that love becomes all the reward you will ever need.

At least until what you set into motion comes full circle and others must also decide to stand up and be counted, or risk disappearing into the fog of history forever...

* * * * *

Look for connected Harlequin Blazes set in the struggling Pacific Northwest town of Earnest, including Troy Metexas's story, later this year.

YOU HAVE TO KISS
A LOT OF FROGS...
Tawny Weber

To Krysta and Melyssa, for still believing
in fairy tales.

To Brenda, for always giving me chances.

And to Lori and Tony, for being so awesome.

Prologue

"SO YOU WANT TO KNOW about the Great Rite, do you?" The woman's oddly accented words were husky, reminding him of lusty mornings after. "Sex is a fabulous source of power. Combined with will and intent, the power is amplified by the Winter Solstice."

"So how's that work? December twenty-first you get up on stage and have sex in front of a bunch of chanting people and call it magic?" Sebastian Lane clarified. He'd got that much from his research, but wanted her take on it. What made people believe in this…stuff?

As if she read his mind, the blonde tilted her head and gave him an indecipherable look. "The magic is real. And the results are always… amazing."

Her sultry once-over suggested she'd be happy to give him a personal lesson right there on the cold steel of the noisy nightclub table. Once upon a time, it would have been tempting. But Sebastian had learned over the years not to mix business with pleasure.

And thanks to the article his editor wanted, this sexy blonde was all business. Sex business, of course. That's what Garret always assigned him. Sebastian's way with woman was something of a legend at *Machismo* magazine. A legend that was rapidly getting in the way of his career goals.

Who knew he'd finally get tired of being seen as a sex object.

"I believe in the power of sex, don't get me wrong. But what I'm really interested in is what makes people believe that sex has some form of magical power," he said carefully, not wanting to lead her response. Or, he admitted to himself, to show his cynicism. Witches, magic, bullshit. It was all smoke and mirrors. And it was his job to report the story, to blow through the smoke to the truth.

Sebastian had made a name for himself in sex, building his reputation on breaking sex scandals. Pornography, prostitution, politicians. The standards, he called them.

"Oh, believe me," the woman repeated, her husky voice intent over the loud music, "the magic is just as real as the sex."

Was this a head game, or did she really believe that? Only one way to find out. Sebastian leaned forward, giving her his most charming smile. Her swift intake of breath, the dilation of her pupils and the fact that she didn't pull back told him he had her.

He arched his brow and challenged, "Show me."

After a long, considering look she slid to her feet and gestured for him to follow her through the crush of bodies.

"I know your work," she said, glancing over her shoulder. Her words were quiet, but he could still hear them over the pounding music and loud voices. The nightspot, Mystique, was purported to be a witches club, from the high priestess–styled servers to the pentacle engraved on the dance floor. What better place, his editor had prodded, to gather feedback for a feature story on the Great Rite. Sex magic—fluff at its best.

"It's always good to have the work recognized," Sebastian returned, paying more attention to the sales menu than her words. Love spells, money spells, fertility spells. Looked like Garret was right. There was a bundle to be made in witch-world.

"Your articles are…interesting," she continued, sweeping a curtain open with one red-taloned hand. "It's a shame a man of your talents shows so little respect to women."

Already playing with the angle of his opening paragraph, Sebastian followed her into the hazy, incense-filled room. Shock rocked his body, even though he'd never admit it. Holy shit. This was…wild. Wall-to-wall bodies, proving that group sex was, apparently, good sex. Finally, he tore his gaze from the room, with its black walls and flickering candles shadowed by the multiple couples having sex on every surface—horizontal and vertical.

Even he, as sexually adventurous as he was, was a little shocked. Then her words sank in. He smoothed out his frown.

"Respect?" His mellow tone didn't reflect his irritation. He totally respected women. They were, in his mind, the most amazing creatures on earth. He hoped to devote his entire life to studying, appreciating and enjoying them.

"You use women," she said, her voice low and even. But there was a snap underneath the soft words. "You use them in that magazine you write for. That men's rag that denigrates women."

Ignoring the sounds of sex-gone-good, Sebastian tilted his head to one side, trying to determine if she was kidding. She'd known he wrote for *Machismo*. She'd enthusiastically agreed to be interviewed.

"Sweetheart, I'm doing an article on the Great Rite," he reminded her. "If you want to back out of our interview, that's your call. Don't make it personal."

"It's never personal to you, is it, Mr. Lane?"

For the first time since he'd stepped into Mystique, Sebastian felt an inkling of discomfort. Tension wound a tight noose around his spine. The last time he'd felt like this, he'd been staring down the wrong end of a sawed-off shotgun, trying to break a story on a prostitution ring fronting as a tutoring center.

But this woman had no weapon. And from what he could tell, nobody else in the room was paying any attention to them.

"Sweetheart, letting things get personal is what causes problems in my business," he told her as he shifted to the balls of his feet.

"And when it's not business?" she asked as those red-nailed fingers flicked the buttons of her robe. The heady scent of incense was starting to make Sebastian's stomach churn. One button, two buttons, three. The silky black fabric shifted, then slithered to the floor.

"It's always about business," he said absently, all of his attention suddenly diverted by her quite fine nude body.

She made a hissing sound as she shook her head, sending the slide of white-blonde hair over her naked shoulders.

"Selfish games you like to play, but now it's come, the time to pay. Your pride is great, your talent immense, your ability to wield them I take forth hence." The husky voice rose, throbbing with an intensity that made the hair on the back of Sebastian's neck stand at attention. "Must arrogance depart and your puffed-up ego be blown, this curse will only break when you put a woman's needs before your own."

Light flashed in the dark room, momentarily blinding him. Power surge? Before he could do more than wonder, Sebastian's head did a quick spin. His stomach quickly followed, like he'd fallen off a tilt-a-whirl.

Holy hell. Mom had always told him masturbation would make him go blind, but dammit, he hadn't even had his hands in his pockets.

It was enough to put a guy off sex for a month.

1

JORDAN OLLIVER EYED the oh-so-bad-for-her temptation with a sigh. *Just don't drool,* she warned herself. The last thing she needed was for her gnawing hunger to be obvious. Delicious, decadent and a constant enticement—she hated that it took every ounce of willpower she had to resist the urge to nibble.

In the year she'd been at *Machismo,* she'd developed an overwhelming oral fixation. One that she was forcing herself to deny, since she was sure giving in to it would derail not only her standing at the magazine—such as it was—but also her career plans.

So she dragged her attention off the sleek, tempting sight of tall, dark and sexy—her fellow reporter Sebastian Lane. Instead, she snapped her teeth into a cruller, welcoming the fat-laden sugar rush. It was a lousy substitute, especially since she was up to one a day. If she wasn't careful, she'd gain ten pounds. Or worse, get sick of donuts, dive across the table and take a big, juicy bite out of Sebastian.

She wasn't sure which bothered her more. Her fascination with Sebastian, or her resentment of him. The Golden Boy. Always two steps ahead of everyone else, he was the magazine's star. And her father's idea of the perfect son.

"Olly, I need you to revise this article," Randolph Garret,

Machismo magazine's editor, said, diverting her attention even more successfully than the deep-fried pastry. He tossed a folder across the table at her.

She frowned. First at the folder, then at Garret. "Revise it? Why? You wanted an article on what to get a woman for Valentine's Day, right? That's what I wrote."

Garret gave her his patented, don't-forget-who-you're-talking-to look. One blond brow arched over narrowed blue eyes. He didn't say anything, just waited.

Jordan had to grind her teeth to keep from voicing a smart remark. She was here at *Machismo* to prove a point. If she could succeed here, at a men's magazine publication, the magazine's owner—aka her father—would be forced to accept that she was serious. Then he'd be forced to see her as an actual asset instead of a pretty little princess to be indulged. Which meant keeping her snide comments to herself.

"The article needs a little different slant. Why don't you look at my notes, see what you think," Garret instructed, indicating the folder.

She didn't bother to open the file.

"You want a fairy tale. Fiction rather than fact," she guessed. "Something that feeds men's prurient fantasies that their girlfriends really like wearing scratchy lace merry widows while cooking chicken fingers and serving frothy mugs of beer."

"That's what our readers want," he reminded her. Jordan shrugged, but before she could agree Garret turned with a big grin to ask, "Right Sebastian?"

The last of the donut squished between her fingers. This, more than the fear of rejection, was what kept her desire to nibble her way up Sebastian's torso at bay. No matter what she did, how hard she tried, she'd never be as good as the

Golden Boy. She looked at *Machismo's* shining star and her father's favorite reporter. If it wasn't for his easy humor and the fact that she knew he wasn't trying to undermine her, she might hate him for that alone.

Instead, she told herself to pretend he didn't exist. Or when that didn't work—she tore off another bite of donut—she found other oral compensations.

"Every story's got a variety of slants," Sebastian said reluctantly, shifting his attention from the window he'd been contemplating. Weird. He was usually the life of these meetings, tossing around ideas and flirtatious comments with equal enthusiasm. Jordan frowned, noting for the first time the stress tightening the corners of his eyes.

For a second, she had the urge to climb over the table and give him a hug. But unlike the other four women in the room, she'd never been the groupie type.

Well, that and if she tried, her father would go into overdrive to ensure the Golden Boy was hooked good and strong. Sell off his youngest daughter to net his dream son? In a heartbeat. No, thank you. Someday, she'd have success, her father's approval and a hot sexy guy's attention. And none of them, dammit, would have anything to do with the other.

In the meantime, she took another bite of the donut.

"Right, right. There's always a slant," Garret agreed heartily with Sebastian as he paced the room. "But I'm asking what slant you personally would go for."

Sebastian grimaced. She wasn't sure if it was because he ended up sucked into every decision, as if his agreement represented a gold star of approval. Or if it was whatever had put those stress lines on his forehead.

"For *Machismo,* the obvious is probably better," he said, giving Jordan a look that said he was sorry, but she should already know this. "Men aren't deep thinkers. If you can find a way to tie in the article to one of the sponsors' products, say the Twisted Knickers Lingerie? Extra points."

Jordan knew he was right. She hated it, but she had to start using that fact. While *Machismo* catered to men, it wasn't an in-your-face chauvinistic magazine. It was more along the lines of a good-ole-boy club on glossy paper. Which was why she'd nagged her father into letting her work here, specifically.

Because if she could make it here, he'd have to admit she could make it anywhere.

With that in mind, she patted the folder and gave Garret her best smile. "More cheesy fantasy, less reality. A sprinkling of hardcore client ass kissing on the side. Got it."

Garret's lips twitched, but he just went on to deliver the next article revision. Jordan tuned it all out, focusing instead on jotting down revision ideas. As soon as Garret wound up the Thursday afternoon editorial meeting, she gathered her notepad and the folder and hurried for the door.

She told herself it was so she could get this article rewritten before noon and still have time to work on her column proposal.

It had nothing to do with wanting to avoid being alone in the room with Sebastian.

Despite her efforts, she and Sebastian reached it at the same time. Shoulder to shoulder, they looked at each other. She raised her brow, hoping he'd take the hint and hurry up. He just grinned.

"You know, I wouldn't ask you to wear scratchy lace while you were cooking my chicken," he murmured. "I'd hate for anything uncomfortable to irritate that alabaster skin of yours. I'm such an easygoing guy, I'd let you cook in the nude."

Her heart pounded so hard she was sure it would leap through her businesslike button-up shirt and splatter on her toes. Jordan struggled to keep her breathing smooth and her expression amused. As if the idea of the Golden Boy talking about her and nudity in the same sentence didn't make her want to nibble her way down his washboard abs.

Was he flirting with her? Should she check his temperature? Acting as if nothing was out of the ordinary, Jordan gave him a sweet smile and leaned closer to lie. "I have about as much interest in getting nude with you as I do in posing that way for the cover of *Machismo*."

"You'd make one helluva cover, princess," he said, his tone husky and his eyes heating as he dropped his gaze to inspect her body.

Holy cow, he was flirting with her. Thinking about her. Naked. Images of him seeing her nude filled her mind in blazing Technicolor. Her body went into instant meltdown. Heat poured through her system, beading her nipples beneath the crisp cotton of her blouse and sending damp awareness to pool between her legs.

He must be ill.

Forcing herself to keep her cool, though, Jordan rolled her eyes. And, with no hint at the spark of delight shivering down her belly, brushed past him. The scent of his cologne, clean and fresh, filled her senses. Her shoulder skimmed the hard planes of his chest, tingles adding to the melting desire already working through her system.

"Everybody at the Monday morning meeting," Garret called out. "I'll have some personnel changes to announce as well as who's getting the new column."

Jordan automatically crossed her fingers and sent up a wish.

"Hey, Lane, do you have a minute? You haven't turned anything in for the column yet and I want to run some ideas by you."

At Garret's words, Jordan almost tripped over her own practically shod feet. What? No! She wanted to object. Dammit, that column should be hers. Her What Women Really Want column was perfect. For her, and for the magazine. She'd done enough research, included all the statistics to support her idea. And she'd even thrown in the cheesy sluttiness slant for advertising.

Donut churning in her stomach, she jutted out her chin and determined to do whatever it took to make her column the winner. Somehow, someway, this time she was going to come out on top of Sebastian Lane.

GOD, HE WAS SLIPPING. Sebastian watched Jordan Olliver stride away, her clipped, controlled pace not disguising the sway of her hips. He'd never met a woman he didn't love watching walk away.

Except Jordan. Her, he always had the urge to call back. An urge he was careful to squash like an irritating fly. Despite many hours mulling over why, he just couldn't figure out what it was about her that fascinated him. It wasn't her sense of style, since she dressed in an uptight way that did nothing to show off her curves. Her brown hair was short, flippy and streaked with coppery strands that caught the light whenever she turned away. Which was often.

And if there was one thing Sebastian Lane used to pride himself in, it was his gift with women. How to woo them, how to do them, how to leave them smiling and waving goodbye. And how to know which ones to stay the hell away from.

At least, that'd been something to be proud of up until four weeks ago. Before his life had gone to hell.

But even without the bitter irony, he'd never have chased Jordan. Thanks to her daddy, she was strictly off limits.

"C'mon into my office, Lane. We need to talk."

Pulled from his contemplation of Jordan's butt, Sebastian followed with a sigh. Garret was a good guy. Wickedly clever and savvy in the ways of getting the most from his staff. But that tone, the serious-boss edge to it, told Sebastian this little talk didn't bode well for his currently miserable state of mind.

"Have a seat," Garret said, gesturing to the chair opposite his desk. Sebastian gathered the stack of folders and magazines and, looking around, dumped them on the TV stand, then dropped into the chair.

"You know you're the best reporter we've got," Garret started. Sebastian could tell the editor was going for the slow build, so he slid a little lower in the chair and crossed his feet at the ankles. "Your work covers the gamut—anything with the human element, especially anything that hints at sex, and you nail it three ways from Sunday."

"I'm good for more than sex," Sebastian protested, unwilling to admit just how vitally true that statement was. Especially since he currently sucked at sex. And not in a good way. "I told you last month, I'd really like to refocus. To cover topics other than sex for a while."

"Sure thing. You're *Machismo'*s biggest star. And we expect you to grow even bigger. Huge, actually."

Huge. Sebastian forced back his sardonic laugh in order to hide the touch of hysteria. He hadn't grown huge in weeks. Four freaking weeks as a matter of fact. His nine-inch glory days were apparently over.

Sure, he could still get it up. But every time, up was about a quarter inch less than the last. Hell, at this rate with a few more hard-ons, there'd be nothing left to grow. And once he was up? Nothing. Nada. He couldn't maintain those ever-shrinking inches to save his life. Or his ego.

Thanks to that bitch…er, witch.

"I hate to say it, Lane, but your performance has been lacking lately."

Understatement of the year.

"Mr. Olliver even called this morning. He's wondering if you aren't stimulated enough."

Sebastian winced. If he tried any more stimulation, he was pretty sure his dick would fall off.

"I'm fine. I've just got a lot going on."

"Why don't you take tomorrow off, make it a three-day weekend? Take a break, grab one of those women who're always falling all over you, go have a good time."

As if.

"I'm fine. I don't need time off."

"Look, Lane. Sebastian…" Garret sighed and leaned forward, his hands folded together on the only clear space in the office, the center of his desk blotter. "Mr. Olliver and I want to do whatever it takes to get you back on top of your game. But you haven't been yourself lately. Hell, you haven't even turned in that article on bogus sex magic you were supposed to write a couple weeks ago."

Sex magic. Nothing bogus about it.

Sebastian struggled against the need to tell Garret everything. The witch. The curse. The impotent misery. Even though he was gossiped over and teased about being a ladies' man, Sebastian had a deep, intense respect for women. Which meant he never talked about his relationships, whether they lasted an hour or a month. So this sudden urge to share was unfamiliar. And hellishly uncomfortable.

Unable to stand it any longer, he leaned forward, his elbows on his jean-clad knees, and puffed out a breath. Then, in a low tone, he asked his editor, "What if that magic stuff is real?"

"Huh?"

"What if the magic is real? What if they do get naked, have sex, cast spells. But not the mumbo jumbo kind. The real kind. The take-a-guy's-manhood-and-turn-it-into-a-limp-noodle kind."

Swallowing the anger that'd lodged in his throat, he forced himself to remember that night. The smell, the bodies, the words.

The miserably real results.

Results nobody was going to believe.

"Beg pardon?" At the shocked expression on Garret's face, Sebastian forced himself to wink, as if he'd been joking. After a couple stunned seconds, Garret laughed uncomfortably.

"Look, Lane, you've been on the fast track for a while. You've been working hard. Top-notch, of course. But maybe you need a break."

A break? Like that was going to help. Wasn't he already broken? Oh, sure, after his little run-in with the crazy witch with the grudge, he'd figured it'd been a joke. But he'd had a date the next night and, like most of his dates, it'd ended up back at her place. Angi had been hot and horny. They'd gotten naked fast and started playing slip and slide. Hard and happy, he'd headed for home. Then, poof, nothing. He just... couldn't. His dick just...wouldn't.

Garret continued, "We're kicking up the magazine's circulation goals. We need you performing at your best."

His best? Hell, he hadn't even been able to perform at his worst. After the failed date with Angi, he'd tried a few more times, a few other women. Then he'd become worried that maybe the witch's spell might be, well, real. He'd tried to remember her words. Something about letting the woman go first. But he'd never had a gal not come, so it should have been an easy fix.

"The sales team is hitting some top dogs this month," Garret continued. "Olliver wants to take it to the next level, to take *Machismo* from regional to national. Quantity and quality. We need our heavy hitter in top shape to make it happen, though."

Heavy hitter, hell. Five women, all of them left with earth-shattering orgasms thanks to his skill with his fingers and tongue. But him? He was left with jack diddly. Sebastian shoved a hand through his hair, frustration making him want to rip it out by the roots.

He'd finally gone over the edge last night. Obsessed with the wording of the curse, he'd figured he had to take it further than just letting his partner come first. So he'd hooked up with this chick, very demanding. He'd figured, hey, maybe that's what it'll take. A bossy one. He winced at the memory of the buxom brunette telling him to drop drawers, that she got off spanking guys. Hell, he'd actually had his jeans unzipped before his brains had reengaged.

God, he was getting desperate.

"Lane, seriously. If there's anything I can do, just say so. I'm here for you, man."

But not desperate enough to share his misery.

"I'm fine," he said again. "I just need to get a few things... straightened."

And keep them straight, dammit. Unable to take any more, Sebastian slid to his feet. He had to get out of here. The combination of stress, sexual frustration and the memory of how close he'd come to hitting on Jordan, of all women, was enough to make him crazy.

"We need you in top form next week," Garret reminded him, the frown in the guy's watery blue eyes making him look like a drowned basset hound. "You're a part of the sales pitch meeting on Wednesday. I want total focus, okay? And I want that sex article. It's the feature of the next issue and we need time to get it polished before the presentation."

"Sure," Sebastian agreed, not really caring. Maybe he'd better start paying more attention, he chided himself. After all, it was starting to look as if his career was all he had. His favorite pastime wasn't doing so good. "I think I'll take you up on that break offer, though. I'll take tomorrow off, head out of town. I have to do a little more research, but I'll get the witch article to you by Monday."

"At the latest," Garret agreed reluctantly, his smile gone now. Late articles didn't make for a happy editor. "That reminds me, though. Olliver tossed his weight behind your name for the new column. I need an actual proposal though."

He'd been the one to suggest the column two months ago, wanting a platform to prove he could write about more than sex and how to hook the ladies. Cursed, now it meant more than ever. And, he shuddered, it might be all he had left to be proud of.

"I'll have it to you this afternoon," Sebastian promised. Then he remembered a flash of something in a pair of caramel-brown eyes at this morning's meeting and frowned. "Who else is in the running?"

"Tomlin on sports, Cransfield for electronics and Marley mentioned a business angle. Stocks, investments, juggling funds."

The tight knot of tension loosened for the first time in two weeks. Okay, if he couldn't have sex, at least he'd have his career.

"Oh, yeah," Garret remembered. "And the princess."

The princess. Jordan, of the sexy eyes and even sexier mouth. The woman who haunted his dreams, even now that those dreams had gone from wet to pathetically dry. Randall Olliver, the king of periodicals' gorgeous, smart-mouthed daughter. Damn. The last thing he wanted was to go up against her.

By Sebastian's third year at *Machismo,* Olliver had made it clear he saw the younger man as his protégé. The potential prince to his kingdom. Both flattering and tempting for a boy from poor beginnings. Then he'd been introduced to Jordan, and Olliver had hinted that princedom had some sweet perks. As tempting as Jordan was, Sebastian had regrettably had to decline. Olliver might be willing to use his daughter, but Sebastian wasn't. No matter how much he wanted her.

Because if ever there was a woman to get a guy hard and horny, Jordan was her.

2

"SHIT."

Sebastian's pride and joy hit yet another ugly rut in the miserable excuse for a road. Fists clenched on the Corvette's steering wheel, he struggled to keep the lean, mean machine from going off a tree-infested cliff.

What was a city boy doing in the freaking woods? He should have refused Olliver's offer to use his cabin to get away and relax. Sebastian could have stayed in his apartment, researched until he found an answer to this curse. Except that he'd been afraid if he stayed in the city, he'd do something crazy.

Like try and have sex. Again.

And one more failure just might kill him. But at least if his car faced it into a tree, he'd understand why. This curse? He just didn't get it. He was always respectful of women. Sure, he'd slept with quite a few wonderful ladies. But he'd never got naked with a woman he didn't like. Of course, he'd yet to figure out if any of them actually liked him back, or just liked what he could do for them.

He didn't figure that made him a cynic. Just a sucker who'd been burned enough to know that he'd have to pay to play. Since he couldn't conceive of life without the blessed benefits of the opposite sex, he accepted the costs.

But he'd never thought he'd pay like this. Cursed and

unable to find a way to reverse the damn thing. Some investigative reporter he was. Sure, he'd figured out who the woman was and why she'd held such a grudge. The bartender had vividly recalled her ranting about the series Sebastian had written on women who used men. But Uma, no last name, had gone underground. Just disappeared, and nobody at the club claimed to know her. Short of trying to convince the cops that some pissed-off woman who didn't like his writing had cursed his willie to shrivel, Sebastian was stuck.

He'd tried everything he could think of to break the curse. He'd focused on "putting her needs before his own" with every freaking woman. The results? It was only getting worse. He wasn't a selfish man, but dammit, four weeks of almost constant sexual foreplay and not a drop of personal satisfaction? It was like some perverted version of hell.

One more turn, a dozen swear words, and the potential of becoming airborne as his prized classic '66 Corvette flew over a pit, and there it was.

Olliver's cottage. Like everything the publishing mogul owned, calling it a cottage was a major understatement. Three stories high, balconies wrapped around like a ribbon and a bank of plate-glass windows gave it more of a château in the redwoods appearance than that of a mountain cabin.

For a brief moment, Sebastian was tempted to rest his head on the steering wheel. But that would have been just one more sign of weakness, and he was pretty much tapped out in that area.

He glanced in the rearview mirror and noticed the freckles across his nose were growing. The only thing on his body with the power to increase, apparently. The first one had appeared the morning after his little encounter with witchy poo, with a new one every day since. And with each new freckle that grew, his dick shrank.

With the same determination he'd used to pull himself out of the slums of L.A., he sucked up the self-pity and climbed out of the car. Straightening his shoulders, he promised himself when he took that hell-ride back down the mountain, he'd have a game plan. He eyed the ever-widening black puddle dampening the dirt under the front end and could only shake his head. He must have punctured the oil pan on that last rock.

Figured.

Not able to dredge up enough energy to care, he grabbed his duffle and laptop bag from behind the seat and strode up the flower-lined path to the front door. Fishing around in his pocket for the key, it wasn't until he reached the front steps that he noticed the lights on inside.

He glanced around, noting that there were no other cars anywhere.

At the front door, he heard the noise—crashing sounds, like an animal or a clumsy burglar.

Adrenaline drowned out exhaustion as Sebastian's senses hit full alert. Moving with slow precision, he leaned down to set his bag on the wide-planked porch floor as he slid the house key out of his pocket. A quick snick and the lock opened.

The noise didn't abate. Grateful that Olliver's fancy-assed house came with well-oiled hinges, Sebastian slipped quietly down the hallway. He briefly recalled his cell phone, tossed in the console of the 'vette.

His back to the wall, he edged his way toward the open door at the end of the hall and all the noise. With a deep breath, he turned and leaped through the doorway into the semidark room. The dim hall light glinted off metal as a hammer arced, midswing.

Sebastian growled, diving forward to grab the figure by the upraised arm and tackle him to the floor. A screech temporarily deafened him, then the intruder's body bucked, like a wild horse, beneath him. He snagged the guy's arm before it could send the hammer into his skull, tugging the tool away and tossing it behind him.

He grunted as an elbow jabbed him in the eye. Stars exploded painfully. Pissed, he anchored the body with his hips and cussed. It took another thirty seconds before the stars faded from his vision and he realized the squirming figure pressed against his groin was actually female.

Figured.

Then she smacked him in the ear.

"Cut it out," he ordered with a growl, dropping his body to lay flat against hers and quickly catching both hands over her head before she swung at him again.

Her struggles grew frantic. God, what a wild woman.

"I'm not going to hurt you," he ground out, trying to reassure her as he strained to keep his hold.

She stilled. Panting, her breasts pressed in miserable temptation against his chest, making him painfully aware of how well her curves fit beneath the hard length of his body.

"Lane?"

Huh?

Sebastian squinted through his one good eye, trying to make out the woman's features. The meager hall light didn't reach them here on the floor. He risked the rest of his sight and leaned closer.

Doing so pressed him tighter against those glorious curves. He almost groaned at his body's reaction. Instant heat. The hard, oh-yeah-you-like-this kind of heat. His nostrils flared. His pulse sped up. His dick, bless it for trying, hardened.

With one eye, he glared at the woman's face in the dim light.

Shit.

"Princess?"

"Don't call me that," she snapped. Her voice wasn't as clipped as usual. She sounded more breathless, probably due to his throwing her on the floor and pinning her there.

Pinning her. As in, he was lying flat on top of his boss's daughter, manhandling a coworker and seriously pissing off a woman who always looked at him as if he was a slimy toad. All at the same time.

If he let her loose, he figured she'd probably beat the hell out of him. He couldn't stay pressed against her warm, tempting body, though. That was pure masochism.

"What are you doing here?" he asked, carefully shifting to one side so his leg was still wrapped over her body, but his weight was resting on his side on the hardwood floor.

"This is my cabin."

"Olliver's cabin," he corrected absently.

"Duh," she growled breathlessly. "I'm an Olliver."

Right. He knew that. His brain was obviously on a trip south of his belt. Sebastian shrugged, muttering, "I forgot."

"Do you want to get the hell off me?" she asked, her tone snide now. "Or are you planning to give me a little personal peek into your rumored sexual brilliance?"

God, wouldn't that be a pleasure. He'd like to start with that gorgeous, wild mouth of hers and spend half the night teaching her other things to do with it besides smart off at him.

As always, he told himself to pull his mind out of his pants when it came to Jordan.

Much harder to do when she was lying beneath his body. Oh, the reasons were all the same. She wasn't some do-me-and-leave-me gal. Despite her mouth, she was a good girl. The kind who deserved a guy who'd stay past breakfast. Besides, she was his boss's daughter, a rival journalist and from the way she acted, she hated his guts.

But none of the reasons mattered much when her lush body, unfettered by her usual repressed outfits, was pressed against his gloriously hard dick.

A dick that would shrink to the size of a tadpole the minute he made a move. And didn't that ruin the mood faster than an ice-cold shower.

Sebastian wanted to beat the floor in frustration. He was up here to solve his problem, not add another layer of suffering to it. How the hell was he supposed to research with Jordan there? Given how competitive she was, and how unfairly she was treated at work, he was sure if she had an inkling, she wouldn't hesitate to announce his situation on the front cover of *Machismo*.

That's what he'd do.

Knowing that, and Jordan, he bypassed defense and went on the offensive. "What are you doing here?"

"GETTING JUMPED, apparently," she muttered.

God, she was one sick puppy. When she'd realized it was Lane pinning her between his rock-hard body and the miserably solid floor, she'd gone from terror to lust in two seconds flat. The excitement zinged through her system, making her thighs quiver and her nipples tighten.

Furious with her body for reacting so predictably, Jordan glared up at the man straddling her. The backlight from the hallway made him look huge. Not as huge as he'd felt against her thigh, though. Her gaze traveled down his body to his belt-buckle. And the intriguing swelling beneath it.

Her fury ebbed, interest taking its place. Well, well. After a year of either ignoring her or treating her like an irritating little kid, it looked as if she was finally getting hottie playboy Sebastian Lane's attention.

And from the tight thrust of his clenched jaw, he didn't like that idea. Well used to irritating the men in her life, Jordan shrugged off his attitude. More important was how she felt about this very growing…development. Hot, intense desire flashed, warm and tingly through her body, assuring her that she was definitely intrigued.

Nothing new there, though. She'd gotten turned on watching the guy sharpen a pencil before. The real question was, now that he'd proved he could return the interest, what did she want to do about it?

Her body screamed for her to strip naked and jump his bones. The practical, ambitious side of her warned that'd be the stupidest thing she'd ever done since she'd waved the red flag in front of her father's face by telling him that she'd prove her worth as a reporter at his toughest publication.

"I didn't mean to hurt you," Sebastian apologized quietly, looking shamefaced. "I thought you were a burglar or something."

"And yet, you're still on top of me," she pointed out.

"Shit," he muttered, jumping to his feet so fast the rush of air fluttered her hair around her face.

Why was he here? The cabin was about as far from his posh San Francisco lifestyle as it was possible to get and still be paid for with her father's money. Yet here he was, trapping her on the floor.

Now that reality—and the lack of him on top of her—had dulled the sharp edge of her lust, she realized her entire body was screaming in pain. She'd be covered in bruises within the hour. She shifted, wincing as both her butt and her knee protested.

It was her scheduled weekend at the cabin. She'd counted

on the peace and privacy to immerse herself in her favorite form of distraction—creating mosaics—instead of stressing over Garret's column. The last thing she needed was anyone or anything that reminded her of *Machismo* and the suspicion that she was wasting her time there.

That was why she was there. She wanted to ask why he was, but she wasn't stupid.

"Did you come up here on your own? Or is my dad joining you at some point?" she asked, pushing herself up from her prone—and therefore weak—position and checking her scraped knee.

"Just me," he started to say. Then he glanced down.

"Are you bleeding?" he asked, a concerned frown creasing his forehead as he bent lower to assess the damage.

"Damn, I'm sorry. Like I said, I thought you were a burglar or…" He trailed off and looked around, squinting at the opened crates of various colored dinnerware. He frowned at the table, where she'd been hammering a bright purple plate into shards. "A hammer-wielding lunatic with a grudge against dishes?"

"You're lucky I didn't use that hammer on your head," she snapped. "What are you doing here? Why didn't you knock or something?"

"I heard the crashing sounds and thought there might be a problem."

"Of course you did." As always, Sebastian to the rescue. Her? If she'd heard noises, she'd have hightailed it back to her phone and called the sheriff to come check. But not him. Oh, no, he had to break in, ruin her weekend and screw up her project. She had only two more purple plates left.

"What's with the dishes?" he asked.

"Working off some frustration," Jordan muttered, struggling ungracefully to her feet. Her knee protested. Trying to ignore the painful throbbing, she tossed the hammer onto the workbench next to the half-moon frame she planned to cover in broken dishware. In the end, it'd be a hall table with iris flowers, perfect for her aunt's birthday. Next month. Which meant she had to get it finished.

"You need to leave," she told him. She couldn't work if he was here. Hell, she couldn't think if he was here. "This is my weekend. The entire family books their time a year ahead, including guest days."

Sebastian was shaking his head before she even finished talking. "Your dad offered me the place for the next few days."

Her jaw clenched. Of course he had. It didn't matter that it was her time. It never did to her father. Shoulders rigid, she stomp-limped into the kitchen, turning the overhead light on with a slap of her hand.

She felt rather than heard Sebastian follow her. He was awfully light on his feet for such a big guy. A fact that she blamed for his sneaking up on her.

"You call this a cabin?" he muttered, looking around. "Where's the wood stove? The cast iron? The, you know, nod to rustic living?"

Jordan snorted. "My father, go rustic? Hardly."

Sebastian strode across the Italian tile floor, past the chrome appliances and glass-topped table. He stopped at the wide bank of windows overlooking a small, manmade lake. "Getaway country atmosphere, with all the comforts of a modern high rise."

"My sisters' idea of roughing it is the single-head showers upstairs," Jordan said dryly.

"One of your sisters decorated?"

Jordan nodded. "Janine, sister number four. She was playing at it until Daddy found her the right husband."

Sebastian turned away from the view and gave her a long, curious look. The intensity of it made her feel naked. "How many sisters do you have?"

"I'm number five, the youngest," she admitted with a shrug.

As if being labeled by a number hadn't doomed her to always being last. Just like her father giving her his father's name—the perfect son's name he'd been saving through four other daughters—wasn't a sign that he'd finally given up.

Maybe she should start writing fiction instead of reporting facts. She obviously had a knack for it.

"Ahh, yes, the five dancing princesses," he said with a wicked grin, pulling out a chair and making himself comfortable.

Jordan ignored the way his jeans molded to his thighs as he sat, instead shoving her hair out of her eyes and glaring. "That's twelve princesses. And I don't dance."

"Never?"

His look was innocent, but the underlying sexual innuendo was anything but. Jordan just crossed her arms over her chest and stared.

"Why are you here?" she asked.

"I…needed a break. Your father suggested I use his place for the weekend."

"Too bad. I'm using it this weekend," she shot back, planting her hands on the counter and leaning forward. It wasn't until his golden green eyes dropped and heated that she remembered she was wearing a loose, white, peasant-style dress. And nothing else.

She sucked in a breath. His eyes narrowed. The room got warmer. Jordan wanted to fan her flushed cheeks, but he didn't need any more ammunition.

"You have to go," she told him.

"I can't. My car hit a rock." He shot a disgusted glare out

the window toward where he'd probably parked. She thought of his low-slung sports car and winced. He was lucky he hadn't slammed it into a tree. These were four-wheel-drive roads. "A few dozen rocks, actually. One of them punctured the oil pan. I'm stuck. You should do something about that road, by the way."

"It's supposed to keep people away," she told him with a cold smile. "I was dropped off, so I can't drive you out of here. Why don't you call someone to pick you up? Or a tow truck."

"I'm staying," he stated, his tone final.

She ground her teeth, fantasizing for a brief second about calling her father and getting Sebastian kicked out. But she knew if Dad sent anyone hoofing it down that hill, it'd be her, not the Golden Boy. Besides, she admitted to herself as she eyed the long, sexy hunk of man standing across from her, the last thing she needed to do was give her father ideas about the two of them being here at the cabin together.

"Well, then," she murmured with a resigned shrug, pretending that her stomach wasn't tumbling at the images, most naked and sweaty, flashing through her mind. "I guess we're roommates."

3

"NO WAY. WE CAN'T share this cabin. Olliver promised me peace and quiet," Sebastian protested in an irritated growl, following her up the stairs to the guest room. "How peaceful, or quiet, will it be if you're here?"

Jordan rolled her eyes, not bothering to glance back. Ever since Sebastian had retrieved his duffle bag he'd been pitching the same argument.

"It's a big house," she promised them both as they cleared the landing. She pointed to the hall to the left. "My room is way down there." She pointed to the right. "Yours is over here. We don't even share a bathroom."

"Are you going to do the cooking?" he asked, his voice switching to pure charm. "I mean, if I'm stuck with company, it might as well have some benefits. Of the edible kind, of course. You can cook, can't you? I'm a fan of Italian food, if you want to start with pasta."

Even though she knew he was trying to rile her into leaving, Jordan spun around and poked her finger into his very wide, very hard, very sexy chest.

"I am not here to serve you," she growled. His wicked grin, the one that said "gotcha," only irritated her more. "I'm here to relax. So I suggest you get something straight. This isn't *Machismo* and you're not the Golden Boy here. It's my place and I call the shots. Which means you will quit playing games and trying to egg me into leaving."

"Or what?" he asked, not bothering to hold back his laugh.

"Or I won't give you the network key to get on the Internet," she threatened with a sugary sweet smile.

His grin dropped.

"You wouldn't."

"In a heartbeat."

"That's hitting a man where it hurts."

"Oh, poor baby." Hiding a laugh, she twisted the brass knob on the second door and led the way into the guest room. With one hand, she gestured to the space. "Here you go. Completely private. There's even a lock on the door."

"You know, you could be a little friendlier, princess. I'm not the one making your life miserable."

Jordan froze. Miserable? Sure, she might occasionally be unhappy, frustrated and discontented, but that was hardly miserable.

"I don't know what you're talking about," she dismissed.

"If you're happy, you sure hide it well. I mean, you're definitely good at what you do, don't get me wrong. But you don't get nearly enough credit, never enough respect." He sounded uncomfortable, like stating the obvious was being disloyal to her dad or something. Jordan was reluctantly touched, though. She hadn't realized he'd paid enough attention to notice. Or that he'd care.

"Life should be fun," he declared. "You don't seem to be having much with your job."

"Life isn't a fairy tale. We can't all love our jobs every minute like you do, Lane," she shot back. "Especially those of us without golden status."

"Fine." He frowned, tossing his bag onto the bed and

shoving his hands in his pockets, clearly uneasy that he'd said anything. "You know, I could talk to Garret for you. If you wanted."

Her heart stuttered. Jordan stared, not sure what to say. Never in her life had anyone offered to champion her.

"That's sweet, but I'm okay," she refused with a little shrug. Then she gave him what was probably the first genuine, friendly smile in their relationship. His jaw went slack, as if she'd kicked him in the shin.

Jordan blushed.

"What?" she asked, trying not to sound as defensive as she felt. As soon as Sebastian thought he had the upper hand, he'd go right back to nagging her to leave. "There's only room for one Golden Boy, and you've got that position nailed."

"What a stupid title," he muttered.

Jordan's smile widened. Walking through the room, she made sure he had plenty of towels and blankets. Then she headed for the door.

"What's the matter," she teased. "You didn't know that was your primary designation at *Machismo?* Closely followed by Stud King, of course."

She expected him to laugh. Instead he looked as if she'd punched him in the belly and called him a pansy.

"What?" she asked, her hand on the doorknob. No wonder she always ended up with losers. She obviously didn't know how to talk with men. "I'm not poking fun at your masculinity or anything."

He got this weird look on his face. Almost like panic. Then it was replaced by a set, determined expression that sent a trickle of worry down her spine. Kind of like the kind she got when someone told her she couldn't do something. A look that warned, "Oh, yeah? Watch me."

Brow furrowed, he strode slowly toward her. Jordan didn't know why, but she suddenly wanted to run. Stupid. She wasn't afraid of Sebastian Lane. Except…maybe she was a little afraid of that look on his face. And the way her body reacted to it.

Her thighs quivered. Warmth trickled from her suddenly beaded and aching nipples to deep in her belly. She forced herself to keep breathing normally as he stopped just a few inches from her.

Jordan swallowed, looking up to meet Sebastian's gaze. A wicked glint sparked in his eyes, but beneath it she saw something else. Something edgy. Dangerous. Sexy as hell.

"Is that why you won't leave, princess?" he murmured, planting one hand on the wall next to her head and leaning closer, so the warmth of his body wrapped around her like a silken blanket. "You're wanting to find out for yourself just how studly I am?"

"Yeah, right," she dismissed, shooting for sardonic. Instead, she sounded breathless and needy. It was hard to care, though, with Sebastian's mouth just inches from hers. She stared, noting the laugh lines fanning from those hypnotic eyes and the dark whiskers starting to shadow the sharp edge of his jaw.

"Do you listen to the gossip often? All those whispered reports about how I like it in bed? Whether I'm a traditional, missionary style kind of guy? Or if I play on the kinky side?"

"Who whispers?" she said, her eyes locked on his lips. Smooth, full and enticing, they were right there, tempting her to do something stupid. "The talk about you is done in giggles and shouts. And traditional is the last word associated with your preferences."

"And you're wondering?"

"Only about your stamina."

His grin was fast, appreciative and the final straw for

Jordan. She couldn't stop herself. She ran her tongue over her bottom lip. Just the tip of it.

That's all it took. Sebastian's eyes went from amused to molten. Then he lowered his head. Excitement did a happy sprint through Jordan's tummy, her heart keeping pace. Desire, hot, wild and intense, flamed through her.

Finally!

Like a whisper, his lips brushed hers. Just barely a taste, a hint of the decadent deliciousness yet to come. Her breath lodged tight in her chest. Her heart pounded so hard she was sure he could feel it against his mouth.

Then he pulled back. Eyes closed, he shook his head and turned away. Jordan almost screamed in protest. She wanted her kiss, dammit. It was all she could do not to grab him back as he strode toward the bed.

He sucked in a breath and turned to face her, shoving his hands in his pockets again, as if to hide them away.

"Gossip's a funny thing, princess," he said in a low voice. "Half of it's always lies and nobody ever knows which half. And when it comes to rumors, someone usually gets hurt. I don't want to see you be that someone."

Frustration winding through her system like poison, Jordan could only stare. She had to force herself not to scream. So close, so damned close. A year of lusting after this guy. Of watching and wishing. Of being the only woman at *Machismo* he hadn't hit on.

Fists clenched at her side, she contemplated snagging his arm, yanking him close and taking that damned kiss.

"Look—" he started.

"No harm, no foul," she said, cutting him off. With her stiffest, fakest smile, she shrugged and stepped through the door. "I've got things to do. I'll see you later."

AN HOUR LATER, Jordan had finally gotten a handle on both her frustration and her fury in the best way she knew how.

Cooking.

As always, Sebastian Lane made her yearn for oral satisfaction.

By the time the peppers and garlic were sautéing, she'd narrowed her problem down to one main question. What was she going to do with him?

She was hot for Sebastian Lane, she acknowledged as she chopped broccoli. That barely-there-but-still-melts-your-panties kiss had given her a tiny glimpse of what it could be like with him.

Incredible. Didn't she owe herself incredible?

She laid eight strips of bacon in a second cast-iron skillet and contemplated all the reasons why incredible was a crazy idea.

Sebastian was out of her league. But, as she broke six eggs into a bowl, she mused that she wouldn't mind trading up.

He was her father's idea of the perfect man. The son ole dad had never had and would willingly barter her for in a heartbeat. She whisked the eggs a little harder than necessary, the froth splashing close to the rim of the bowl.

The month she'd started at *Machismo,* her father had hinted that he'd like to see her and Sebastian an item. Then she'd heard through a somewhat questionable source, her oldest sister the gossip queen, that Daddy had guaranteed Sebastian's success at both *Machismo* and any other Olliver Publication. For the small price of marrying his youngest daughter. And hey, Juliette had assured her when she'd gleefully shared the gossip, it didn't even have to be permanent. Just long enough for Daddy to claim Sebastian as his son.

She had to give him credit. Sebastian hadn't taken the supposed offer. For the last year, she'd secretly wondered if it was out of some kind of morality or if he simply wasn't interested in her.

She poured the eggs into the pan and watched them gently bubble as she recalled the look in his eyes when he'd bent down to brush his lips over hers.

He was interested. A little thrill danced low in her belly as she recalled the unmistakable interest in his eyes.

She was interested. She had the tingles to prove it.

She was sure he didn't want her father getting ideas any more than she did, or the people at work spreading gossip.

But—she added vegetables to the omelet—maybe this weekend they could indulge their interest. Here, away from gossip and prying eyes.

The only question was, could she work up the nerve to proposition Sebastian into indulging that interest with her. While nerves simmered in the background, she dished up her version of dinner and reminded herself that she had all weekend.

Whether that was enough time to make a move, or to chicken out, she didn't know.

LURED OUT OF HIDING by the delicious scents, Sebastian stepped into the kitchen and stopped short. He looked at Jordan, her short hair pulled off her face with a pretty ribbon. She'd changed into something that obviously included underwear, thank God. Her blouse was a feminine froth of color, like crushed raspberries, that made her skin glow. To distract himself from his own growing reaction, he looked at the table, set for two.

He offered a hesitant smile. "I was only teasing. I don't expect you to cook for me."

Jordan just raised one brow and asked, "What? You think this is for you?"

He opened his mouth, then shut it. He frowned, looked from her to the table, then shoved his hands in his pockets.

She burst into laughter.

"I'm kidding," she said, giving him a warm smile that made his frown deepen. "Dinner's ready. Have a seat."

"I appreciate this," he told her, not sure if his appreciation stemmed more from his growling stomach or his still-wincing ego, thankful that things hadn't gotten ugly after that kiss upstairs.

She tilted her head to one side and sucked in her bottom lip. Sebastian dropped his gaze to her mouth. He recalled the deliciously sweet taste of that soft mouth. The way her breath hitched, her eyes had warmed. The way his body had reacted, hard and fast. And, he sighed, useless.

He'd ignored his interest in her before, but now, trapped in the mountains, he was finding himself fixated and obsessed. Nice addition to any curse, he had to say.

She came around the counter and he almost groaned. Jeans, tight and worn, cupped her thighs beneath the filmy blouse. Which was the real Jordan Olliver, he wondered. The one who wore girly clothes and beat the hell out of dishware up in the mountains? Who cooked like an angel, if the scents were anything to go by, and teased with a sparkling smile? Or the buttoned-up hardass who fought for bylines, kept her father's name but didn't use his clout and tossed off snarky one-liners with the best of them?

The need to know was driving him crazy.

"Come eat while it's hot," she said.

"What're you up to?" he asked again, crossing to the table and taking his seat. He almost jumped right back up when she reached over and tapped his thigh gently.

"What makes you think I'm up to anything?"

"You're being nice."

"I'm a nice person."

"I hadn't heard that rumor."

"Probably because those wild rumors about you tend to get all the attention."

Sebastian grimaced. Every time she mentioned gossip, he felt like a little boy caught with his hand in the cookie jar. He obviously didn't regret the cookies, but he did wish people would quit talking about them so often.

"Like I said before, rumors are usually exaggerated."

"But based in fact."

"Oh, I don't know. Did you hear the one about Garret and the head of marketing doing it on the copy machine? I've always felt there was little fact to be found in that one."

"Probably because the head of marketing is too short to get on top of the copy machine," Jordan said with a giggle. She actually giggled. Sebastian grinned in return.

"Tell you what," she proposed, leaning forward to rest her elbows on the table and giving him a slow, wicked smile. The kind of smile that said she'd like to do naughty things to his body—it was all he could do not to strip bare, lay on the table and beg. "You give me a chance, despite the rumors. And I'll do the same for you."

He narrowed his eyes. What was she up to? He knew damned well she saw him as one of the main reasons she couldn't get ahead at *Machismo*. So this had to be a ploy of some kind. But he didn't see the catch. And there was always a catch.

Finally, his mouth quirked up on one side and he nodded. "Deal."

Jordan winked, then proceeded to serve the omelet and fruit salad. The next half hour was filled with mouth-watering food and intriguing conversation. Sebastian didn't even realize they'd eaten everything until he looked for his third helping.

"That was delicious," he told her.

She gave him a nervous smile, opened her mouth as if to say something and then shook her head. With a little grimace, she got up from the table, carrying her dish with her.

"I cooked, you clean," she informed him. "You don't mind if I leave you to it, do you? I've got a few things to take care of."

"Things like breaking more plates?" he asked as he carried the platters and glasses to the sink.

"Like I told you before, it's a way to work off frustration," she said with a shrug.

It was all he could do not to suggest some much more pleasurable, naked ways to work off frustration. But he knew what the results would be. Or not be.

Nope, while he'd love nothing more than to feast on her body like a five-course meal, he wasn't about to do it unless he could be in on dessert. He didn't know if it was pride or something else, but he wasn't about to start something with Jordan that he couldn't finish.

So he wished her luck with her crockery destruction and turned to do the dishes. As Sebastian rinsed and loaded the dishwasher, he stared out the window at the sunset, dripping brilliant colors over the mountains. For the first time in four weeks, he felt the tension start to unknot in his neck.

Ten minutes later and one last glance around the sterile kitchen and stunning view, and he congratulated himself on a job well done. He headed for the stairs, but on the way there a flash of color caught his eye.

A mosaic sunset covered the living room wall. Vivid colors melted, one into the other, in a bleeding tribute to the end of day. Sebastian rocked back on his heels, considering the image.

Passion. Power. And if a compilation of broken shards of tile could evoke it, pain.

Well, well. Not only did his favorite smart-mouthed princess wear floaty cotton over a whole lot of sexy skin in private, she was a closet artist.

He wasn't sure which he found sexier.

With a growl, Sebastian stomped down the hall and out the front door. He'd been doing a great job of ignoring his attraction to Jordan. A weekend of enforced company was giving him way too many tempting insights into this sexy woman. Insights he didn't need, considering he couldn't do one damned thing about them. It wouldn't be fair.

He crossed the yard, ignoring the black puddle oozing from under his car as he headed for the relative serenity of the lake.

Seated on a huge rock, he stared out over the calm water and wondered how the hell he'd ended up in this situation. He respected women. Hell, if he was all about the conquest, why hadn't he gone after Jordan despite her father's matchmaking games? She was gorgeous, smart and savvy. Her mouth was almost as enticing for the sass that came out of it as it was for the mobile fullness of her gorgeous lips.

She also had a body that wouldn't quit. He shifted on his perch, his dick growing as hard as the rock under his ass.

He wondered if she secretly wore lacy panties. Or maybe slinky little nighties. The kind with just enough fabric to skim the top of silky golden thighs.

Yeah, if he didn't respect women, he'd have gone for Jordan months ago. He'd have ignored the potential fallout from Olliver, a man who was willing to offer his own daughter as incentive to secure the guy he deemed worthy to run his empire. The empire was tempting, the idea of selling himself and humiliating Jordan wasn't.

And all this obsessing was doing was distracting him from the problem at hand. The damned curse.

Determined to quit wasting time, he shoved all thoughts of Jordan out of his mind and focused instead on trying to figure out how to fix the mess his last big sexual mistake had caused.

Finally, without answers but figuring he had a couple avenues to explore, he headed back up the cabin steps. He saw a small table with a vivid green and blue mosaic pattern. Even though he'd never said so, he'd always admired Jordan's talent.

He just hadn't realized how many different talents she had.

Considering, he let himself in the front door. He'd made it three steps before he realized someone was halfway down the stairs.

A very sexy someone. Slick with a fine layer of oil, Jordan was naked except for a cherry-red towel wrapped over some very intriguing curves, and a wickedly naughty grin.

Talk about talent.

He was so screwed.

4

"OH, NO," SEBASTIAN breathed, a half groan, half protest. "I thought you said you wouldn't disturb me."

The look on his face was a combination of shock, fear and a whole lot of interest. Even as he backed away from the door, his eyes roamed her body, the heat in that look making up for the evening chill as she stood there in her very skimpy, but hopefully sexy layer of baby oil and strategically placed terrycloth.

As Jordan's feminine ego soared, she managed to keep a straight face. "Disturb you? I hadn't said a word. I was just heading out to the hot tub to unwind a little before bed."

If standing at the top of the stairs waiting for him to return for the last fifteen minutes counted as heading out. She'd had second, third and tenth thoughts while waiting. It was crazy to think she could seduce Sebastian. After all, he was a do-'em-if-you-want-'em guy. Hardly the type to need convincing. And if she hadn't seen the interest, the heat in his eyes—or heard his groan and pathetic little excuse about respect— she'd never have had the courage to try to convince him. But this weekend was her perfect chance. Probably her only one, dammit. She'd decided over dinner that she wanted him, but had chickened out on making a move. But a few hours, a few pieces of broken crockery, and she'd worked up the nerve.

And now he was arguing with her.

"Unwind?" he asked, his tone low and just a little suspicious. His eyes were narrowed, intense with desire and appreciation, though, as they wandered over her bare shoulders, down her glistening legs. Her body warmed, tingles shimmering low in her belly.

"Unwind," she repeated in her sexiest tone. "You know, loosen a little tension and maybe even ease some of the pain screaming through my body from that tackle earlier today. And hopefully the water will help reduce the swelling in my knee."

He winced when she turned her leg, showing him the purpling bruise swelling beneath the still-red slash bisecting her knee. The cool draft up her privates from the shifting towel was enough to remind her that she was standing half-naked in the hall for a reason. Sebastian had something she wanted. Jordan told herself to focus on the plan she'd spent the evening perfecting and not the discomfort in reaching it.

"A little dip in the hot tub probably wouldn't hurt you, either," she said, working to sound just this side of disinterested. "You're probably sore."

He frowned, then shifted his shoulders as if testing her words. "How'd you know I was sore?"

"Well, you bitched about the drive enough, it was an easy guess," she said with a smirk.

"And you want me to come into the hot tub with you? To, what? Loosen my muscles?"

Too obvious, Jordan realized. She really sucked at this seduction thing. She just couldn't bring herself to take the blatant, fingers tiptoeing up his chest and flirting with her eyelashes route. So she needed to stick with subtle strategy.

"No biggie," she told him with a shrug that put her towel

in jeopardy. "Your bedroom has a sunken tub with jets. You have plenty of towels and privacy."

She took two more steps down the stairs, close enough for the cool evening air wafting in behind him to raise goose bumps on all her bare parts. She wasn't cold, though. Nerves and the awareness in his eyes were keeping her plenty warm.

"I'll see you in the morning," she added, moving to the side as if making room for him to go upstairs to his lonely tub.

She almost wished he would. Not only because she was having second thoughts, but because then he'd have to brush up against her. And maybe if he did, if his biceps just happened to rub against her towel-covered breast as he moved past, he'd be overcome by lust. Then he'd turn and grab both of her arms in his hands. Push her back against the wall. Lean forward and press his mouth against hers. Kiss her, deep, hot and wild.

Jordan ran her tongue over her suddenly dry lips and huffed out a deep breath. Wow. Maybe she didn't need his actual body. Fantasies were plenty hot, thank you.

A part of her, the part that always pointed, screaming, toward the safest exit, told her to listen. To turn towel and head right back up those stairs. Hot fantasies didn't cost one single bit of embarrassed effort or risk possible rejection. And didn't she already have enough rejection in her life?

Jordan was actually shifting to leave when she realized how conditioned she was to copping out. No. This weekend was about learning to be stronger. How to stand up for herself, to go for what she wanted.

And she wanted Sebastian Lane.

No way she was giving up that easy. Chin lifted, she planted both feet on the stair and crossed her arms over her chest. The towel shifted a scary inch higher. Sebastian's eyes rounded, then narrowed.

"Are you sure this isn't some game?" he asked gruffly. "Maybe temptation in a towel?"

Unsurprised by his insight, Jordan made a show of rolling her eyes and gave a little laugh.

"Oh, please. If I wanted to seduce you, wouldn't I have tried already? When have I flirted? When have I hinted? Shown the slightest interest? Why wait until you're here horning in on my peaceful weekend?"

She kept her breath steady, even though her heart was pounding like crazy as she waited to see if he'd buy that. It'd sounded so good upstairs when she'd practiced it, but now? Said aloud? Totally lame.

He didn't look convinced. So Jordan made a show of heaving a deep sigh that apparently, from the heat in his eyes, did interesting things to her towel.

"What are you worried about?" she asked. "You think I'm going to go back to the office and tell everyone you did something as innocuous as hot tub with me? Are you worried they'll think you sacrificed your principles and got hot and wild with the boss's daughter? Or worse, that you didn't? I thought gossip didn't mean anything to you."

She held her breath, thinking of her sister's suggestion that Daddy had propositioned Sebastian. Any worries she might have harbored that it was true faded as she looked into his eyes and saw, instead of nerves or guilt, simple frustration.

Sexual frustration.

The same kind she was feeling.

Empowered, energized, and for the first time ever, filled with sexual power, she took that final step off the stairs and, her hand still clutching the towel, moved past Sebastian. Just as she reached the hallway, she shot him her sexiest look over her bare shoulder and said, "Or, like everyone else, are you afraid of my daddy?"

She grinned at his scowl, then headed down the hall, her swinging hips making the terrycloth flutter. Enticingly, she hoped.

By the time she reached the door off the kitchen that led to the wide redwood porch spanning the back of the house, she heard his footsteps. She took her time turning on the stereo, then pouring a glass of wine from the bottle she'd left on the sidebar earlier.

If her hand shook as she raised the glass and she gulped more than sipped, well, he was too far away to notice. But refilling the glass might be a giveaway. So she carried it, almost empty, over to the hot tub, where she used her toes to flip the switch. Seduction or not, there was no way in hell she was bending over wearing just a towel.

"You really do have a hot tub," he murmured from the doorway.

"What? You thought I made it up so I could parade around in a towel?" she teased.

"Of course not," he said quickly, almost as if he was afraid to put the idea of her and deliberate temptation in the same sentence.

"So, what's the deal? Did you decide to join me?" she asked, wishing she'd gone ahead and refilled her wineglass anyway.

"Do you have extra suits?" he asked, glancing around the dusk-washed patio. Like there might be a changing area or something.

"The only person who wears a suit is my dad," she said with laugh.

"I meant swimsuits," Sebastian said with a grin.

"So did I."

Jordan took a deep breath and, biting her lip and doing it quickly before she could think twice, flicked the towel so it unknotted and fell to the deck.

SEBASTIAN ACTUALLY FELT the blood pour from the upper hemisphere of his body, swooshing down in a rush to fill his poor, neglected dick.

Holy shit. She was…gorgeous. He couldn't tear his eyes from Jordan. Slender curves, smooth skin and deliciously long legs that just begged for his kisses. Pert, rounded breasts tipped with dusky rose nipples, pebbled invitingly in the cool night air. The dusting of curls between her legs made his fingers itch to touch. Explore. Feel.

Oh, God.

He gulped.

Then she turned and he couldn't help it. He groaned aloud. Her ass was just as perfect as the rest of her. He watched her step into the bubbling, scented water. The tiny, rational part of his brain urged him to get the hell out of there. Run, fast. The aching, neglected part of his body screamed at him to strip and get in the water already. He knew it'd be pointless, since the curse had rendered him pretty well useless.

But for once, Sebastian didn't care about the end results. He just wanted to touch Jordan. To kiss her. Taste her.

He'd always wanted to.

Without conscious direction, Sebastian's fingers went to the buttons of his shirt. Flicking them open, he stared at the water, wishing for a glimpse of the heaven hiding beneath the dark, bubbling surface. He toed off his shoes, then tossed his shirt over the back of a chair. Walking toward the hot tub, he arched a brow at Jordan.

His hand paused on the zipper of his jeans and he waited for some signal.

She just leaned back against the tile tub wall and spread both arms along the edge. Then she gave him a wicked, I dare you look.

Sebastian's jeans hit the deck so fast her eyes went wide. Then she laughed. The sound, a husky melody, made him almost as hard as the sight of her lush curves had. His boxers joined his jeans and he took that final step of no return.

With a glint of appreciation, her golden brown eyes traced the length of his body, stopping for a long moment on his jutting manhood. She gave a silent whistle, then let her eyes finish the tour all the way to his toes.

"I guess you're right," she said with a naughty little smile. "Gossip is horribly misleading."

"Huh?"

"Well, as popular as the talk of your...gift is around the water cooler, the rumors definitely didn't do you justice."

For the first time since he was fourteen, Sebastian didn't know whether to grin or stammer like a blushing school-boy at the sight of a girl looking at his dick. Of course, just like when he'd been fourteen, he had no idea what it would do, either.

For a guy who'd spent his whole life struggling to be the biggest—so to speak—and the best, it was wildly humbling to stand there and know he wasn't. He'd jumped out of air-planes, been shot at and interviewed a psychotic mass murderer. But he'd never felt so, well, naked.

But Jordan's smile didn't judge. She just looked amused and, yes, his ego was grateful to see, impressed. For maybe the first time since he'd hit puberty, Sebastian wasn't worried about proving himself. As he stepped into the hot, frothing water, all that mattered was paying Jordan back for that sweet look of acceptance.

It wasn't until he was submerged to his waist and moving across the hot bubbles that he saw it. The hint of nerves in her eyes. Brow creased, he wondered briefly when he'd last seen nerves in a woman he was naked with. And if he'd cared.

Maybe he had deserved to be cursed.

"Nice," he commented, trailing his fingers over the water as he sank down to the seat about a foot away from her. "You do this often?"

"Relax in the hot tub?" she asked with an arch of her brow. "Or get naked with a coworker?"

He almost snorted water, his laugh was so deep. Sebastian leaned back, resting his elbows on the ledge, and grinned at her. "How about both?"

"Well there was the time that Nancy in marketing and I were taking that kickboxing class at Duchesse Defense and had to hit the showers afterward."

He smirked. "Not quite what I meant."

"No?" she smiled, wafting her hand through the water between them. He noticed how delicate her fingers were as they came closer and closer to his chest with each pass.

"If we're going to compare gossip, it's only fair that you fill in a few blanks," he told her, giving in to the curiosity that had always nagged at him. He'd tried to chalk it up to reporter's inquisitiveness, but now that he was naked with her, he could admit he was fascinated by Jordan. "My sex life is water cooler news. Yours is a total mystery."

Her smile was pure seductive beauty. Slow, wide and wicked, it dared him to keep talking sex.

"Why don't you fill in the blanks yourself, Golden Boy? You're the star reporter. What do you think?"

Unable to resist, he caught her hand as it passed within inches of his chest. Threading his fingers through hers, he shifted, just a little, to find her leg with his.

Her caramel eyes went huge, then narrowed. He grinned. God, he loved her reactions. Wrapping his ankle around her firm calf, he teased the back of her leg with his toes.

"You know, any good reporter isn't going to listen to rumor," he teased. "He's going to get the facts for himself."

With that and a soft tug, he pulled her buoyant body through the water. Her gasp was barely audible over the jets of the tub, but he saw it and smiled. A slow, sensuous smile that promised this wouldn't be the first gasp she'd give. He planned to make damned sure of it.

As she bumped gently against him, she pressed her hand to his chest. Her damp fingers were trembling, just a little. But enough to remind Sebastian of his stand when it came to Jordan. She was a good girl. Not a do-her-then-pat-her-on-the-ass-on-the-way-out-the-door kind of gal.

Which, combined with his current unfortunate sexual impediment, meant this was about the stupidest idea in the world. His brain scrambled for a way out even as he loosened his hold on her hand.

"Well, I guess we'll see who the better reporter is now, won't we," she said before he could untangle himself.

"Huh?"

"You just admitted you think I'm something of a mystery," she said in a low, husky tone. Her fingers now trailing an enticing, heated path up his chest and over his shoulder.

"Which indicates," she said, her fingers sliding in little swirly patterns down his arm, "that you've thought about me. You've wondered. You've...wished."

Oh, yeah, he was wishing. Big-time. And, he realized with

a silent groan of relief, big was the operative word here. A delicious feeling of hot power poured south, filling and hardening him to fondly remembered lengths.

He shifted on the slick hot-tub seat, reveling in both the feel of Jordan's legs as they slid along his and his body's glorious reaction.

"So why don't you tell me about them," she invited quietly, her finger now tracing a path up the back of his neck.

"Them?" he asked, forcing himself to stay still instead of grabbing her with both hands, hauling her tight against him and wrapping her legs around his waist so he could drive himself into her glorious body.

This was crazy. His mind, that dim voice almost smothered by desire, screamed caution. Almost as if she sensed his doubts, she shifted, placing her hands on his shoulders, her touch sending shock waves through his body. Then, in a move made all the more sensual by the buoyant water, she made his hottest fantasies come true when she pulled herself forward, sliding her legs over his hips.

"Your wishes. Tell me about your wishes," she said in a husky whisper.

"Are you magic?" he asked as he lowered his mouth toward hers. "Are you going to make all my wishes come true?"

"Maybe…" She shifted, lifting herself in the water so he caught just a glimpse of her dusky rose nipples. Sebastian ran his tongue over his suddenly dry lips. With a little grin, Jordan mimicked the move, first rubbing her mouth, whisper soft, over his. Then she slid her tongue over his lower lip and gently sucked and nibbled him into idiocy.

With a groan of surrender, Sebastian reached down to settle his hands on the curve of her hips, his fingers sinking into the sweet softness of her butt. Unable to help himself, he lifted her closer. Weightless in the water, she gave a little mewling sound of pleasure, then she curved her legs, wrapping them tight around his waist and straddling him. He swore it felt almost as good as an orgasm when the friction of her curls swept over the hard, aching length of his dick.

She made a sound of delight, hooking her feet behind his back and pressing, undulating, teasing.

Freaking killing him.

Sebastian groaned.

To hell with it. He didn't give a damn about the risks. All that mattered was feeling Jordan, here in his arms. Tasting her. Pleasuring her.

Even if the results did kill him.

5

SEBASTIAN'S DELICIOUS talent was definitely under-reported by the gossips, was Jordan's last thought before her brain overloaded on pleasure. Her lips slid, soft and sweet, over the delicious fullness of Sebastian's. Open mouthed, sensual. Hinting, but not blatant. The motion was driving her crazy.

As if frustrated by her teasing, though, he growled. He didn't ask for control, he took it and turned her world on its side as his mouth went wild on hers.

He scraped his teeth over her bottom lip, then wrapped his tongue around hers. The dance was intense, fast and wild. Her body went into overdrive at the thrusting power of the kiss. He demanded she keep up, match him thrust for thrust, passion for passion. Her breath shuddered, her body heated.

Needing more, she rubbed her swelling nether lips against the silky length of his dick, mewling in delight at the friction. Still calling the shots, his hands gripped her butt tighter, setting the pace for her undulations. Slow, long slides up and down his belly, teasing her with the promise of his length, hard and huge.

She moaned a soft protest as his hands stopped their kneading caress, leaving tingling shivers behind. But she didn't stop her delicious movements. Need built with every pass. She wanted him inside her. Soon. But this dueling foreplay felt too good to end quite yet.

He trailed his hands up her sides in a smooth, easy move. She held her breath, wondering. Hoping. Her nipples, already beaded in the bubbling water, tightened even more. Teasingly close, his hands trailed over the full sides of her breasts, cupping, weighing. But he bypassed the aching tips. Instead he traced his fingers across her collarbone, up her throat and, with one hand around the back of her neck, he pressed his palm to her cheek in the most romantic gesture she'd ever experienced.

It was all Jordan could do not to whimper and melt all over him like a starry-eyed ingenue, ready to fall all giddy in love with one sweet caress.

Oh, no, she reminded herself. This was all about the sex. Great, mind-numbing, orgasm-screaming sex.

He tunneled his fingers through her hair, cupping the back of her head. He pulled her, weightless in the water, up higher. Her heels slid up the small of his back and she shivered as the cool evening air ripped the warm blanket of sexual fog away. Goose bumps coated her arms and shoulders. Her nipples, now inches away from the heated bubbles, beaded with the chill.

Before she could fully register the change, though, Sebastian let go of her head. His hands first pressed against the outside of her thighs to tighten her legs and secure her in this new position. Then they swiftly slid up her wet, trembling body.

Jordan cried out as his palms warmed her nipples. His hands swirled in slow, gentle circles, rubbing the aching nubs. Each rotation sent a spiral of answering pleasure down her body, tightening the ache between her legs. Needing to touch, to caress, she ran her own hands up and down his arms, cupping the rounded hardness of his biceps with a purring little growl of appreciation.

He shifted, one hand now tracing a line down the center of her body, from between her breasts to her belly button, then back up. His other traced gentle, concentric circles around her areola. The circles grew tighter, smaller, closer. She wanted to scream. To force him to touch her. To give her the pleasure that was just there, beyond the edge of her reach.

Then, as if realizing she was right on the edge of sexual insanity, he flicked the sensitive tip. Her body went stiff. She arched closer, her undulations more intense.

"More," she breathed against his talented mouth.

Golden Boy that he was, he gave her more. His fingers tweaked and tormented her nipple. His other hand swept lower, brushing the curls pressed against his belly. Jordan hated to leave the delicious pressure the hard plane of his stomach offered, but she needed more. She had to have what his fingers promised.

Then he moved again, lifting her just a smidge higher, and pulled his mouth from hers. Jordan couldn't stop her moan of protest. Frowning, she opened her eyes to see the wicked grin on his face before he dipped his head and took her achingly turgid nipple into his mouth.

Unable to look away, Jordan watched his tongue slip out, lapping and circling the pale pink bud. Seeing him only added to the incredible sensations he was evoking in her body. Her breathing sped up, her heart raced. His eyes held hers, the golden green depths mesmerizingly sexy as he refused, just with the power of his gaze, to let her look away. To do anything but fully participate in the pleasure he was giving her.

A part of her wanted to hide, to close her eyes and disengage her brain. Because even though this was exactly what she'd wanted when she'd slicked her body with oil and wrapped up in that little towel, having it scared her.

Magic, once experienced, meant she'd never be the same. And Sebastian's talent was purely magical.

But she couldn't stop, couldn't turn away from the ecstasy he offered. She'd asked for this, dammit. And she was going to enjoy every single, solitary element of it.

Free from the fear now, she held his eyes as she released one of his shoulders. Needing to hold the other to keep from floating away, she lifted her free hand to his face, tracing the stubble-roughed edge of his jaw before smoothing her fingers along his cheekbone then into his thick, silky hair. She pressed gently against the back of his head, silently letting him know she wanted more. More pleasure, more pressure.

She saw the straight, white edge of his teeth before she felt them scrape along her flesh. She watched him watch her, knowing her pleasure was clear in the flush heating her chest, the heavy-lidded delight in her eyes.

So focused was she on his mouth, on the powerful delight he was stirring as he teased her breasts, she barely noticed his other hand. Until he touched her.

Jordan's entire body went stiff. Her mind, unable to take the intense overload to her senses, went blank. Her eyes closed. Her head fell back.

Every single cell in her body was focused on the pleasure he was offering. His mouth sucked the stiff peak of one breast into the hot, wet paradise of his mouth. His hand combed through her curls to part her throbbing lips, tracing a finger along her aching, swollen clitoris. Her hips moved in a rhythm of their own now. Her breath shuddered through her lungs as her fingers clutched, kneaded, his rock-hard biceps.

Panting, she bit her lip to hold back her cries of bliss. His teeth nipped, his fingers swirled. Her mind was blown. Oh, God, he was good.

Then, moving so fast she couldn't stop her scream of

shock, he grasped her waist and lifted, spinning her so her back was against the wall of the hot tub and he was facing her.

Eyes huge, Jordan quickly let go of his arms to brace her elbows on the border of the deck so she didn't slide into the water.

"What—"

He grinned. A wicked, sexually confident smile that said he knew exactly how far onto the edge of crazy he'd pushed her and he was about to send her flying off the other side.

She smiled back, reaching out to wrap her hand around the back of his neck to pull him close. She needed a kiss. And for once, she was sure that she'd get what she needed.

Lips melded together in glorious longing, tongues sliding in a slower dance this time. A dance that promised fulfillment, that swore the ultimate pleasure.

He shifted away. Jordan made a sound of protest. Then, in another of those swift, shocking moves, Sebastian reached down to grip her thighs, lifting them out of the water.

"Hold tight," he warned as he lowered that gorgeous chest into the heated bubbles, anchoring her legs over his shoulders.

Jordan's gasp rang out, drowning out the cricket serenade and echoing through the night air. She splayed her arms to grab the sides of the hot tub. Water sloshed, warm and bitter with the scent of chlorine. Teetering between crazy turned-on and shocked, she did the only thing possible. She laughed.

"Gonna drown me?" she teased.

"Oh, no," he returned, his voice husky and low. "I've got plans for you, princess."

For the first time in her life, that nickname didn't bother Jordan. It made her feel special, beautiful. Desired.

Wanted, even. She swallowed, pressing her lips tight together to hold back the ridiculously overdramatic urge to sob. Her flimsy reasons for luring him here, the silly idea of using him to prove something, fled.

Her heart tripped, but she righted it with a fast reminder that as incredible as he might make her feel, both emotionally and physically, she was the only one with anything on the table. Or on his shoulders, as the case was. Any silly emotions were hers to have and to hide. To do anything else would be unfair to Sebastian.

Completely unaware of the emotional onslaught threatening to drown the flames of passion he'd stirred, Sebastian grinned and slid his hands up the muscles of her wet calves to her thighs, where his fingers tickled a path inward.

He shifted, and with a shrug of his shoulders spread her legs wider, offering an unlimited view of the wet, swollen proof of her desire.

His eyes clouded, a brief look of almost pain flashing across his handsome face. Then, his gaze meeting hers, he offered the sweetest sexy smile she'd ever seen.

"C'mere," he murmured, "I'm starving for you."

SEBASTIAN REVELED in the glorious sight of Jordan's body, spread wide and glistening, waiting for him. God, she was beautiful. So responsive, so real. She was the sweetest thing in the world.

But how sweet? Sebastian had to know.

Mouth watering for a taste, his muscles clenched as he slid deeper into the water. With her ankles resting on his shoulders, Jordan lowered too, so she was floating on the surface, bubbling water frothing around her alabaster limbs.

"Sebastian—"

"Shh," he interrupted. He knew it was crazy. Knew what was at risk. What he couldn't have in the end. But he wanted this moment. To feel it, to experience it fully. There was something magical about the sight of Jordan, her hair all damp and tousled around her beautiful face. Her lips parted, swollen from his kisses. Her eyes glazed with passion.

And her body. His eyes cruised the length of her glorious form, shown to perfection by her vulnerable position. He'd always known she had a hot little body on her. But, oh, man. She was better than even he'd dreamed. And when it came to Jordan Olliver, he'd dreamed a whole hell of a lot.

And now he was going to make the hottest of those dreams come true.

His dick throbbed with excitement, almost painful in its intensity. Even though he knew he wouldn't be using it, it was all he could do not to reach down and pat it in sympathy. His dick had paid private homage to Jordan many a time in his dreams, so he knew how hard—no pun intended—this was.

Concentrating like an artist with his muse, Sebastian traced a delicate line from the inside of Jordan's knee to the glistening temptation between her thighs.

Her eyes flashed with something. Nerves? He wasn't— they closed too fast. Knowing this was all he was going to get, though, he needed that connection. So he pulled his finger away from her juicy womanhood and waited. Slowly, reluctantly, her lush lashes lifted and she met his eyes.

From the tiny crease in her brow, she'd got the message. Smart girl. Her brains were damned near as sexy as her body.

His gaze locked on hers, Sebastian ran one long finger over her swollen bud. She hissed out a breath, her eyes going soft with passion.

Color washed over cheeks, barely visible in the night shadows. He didn't know if it was embarrassment or excitement.

Either way, it only added to her beauty. It only made him want more.

He traced his finger up, down. Her breasts rose and fell. He swirled one finger, then two, just teasing. Her hips lifted, as if begging for more.

Never a man to refuse a lady, he gave her what she was asking for. Intense pleasure. Fingers swirled. In, out, around. Her hips began that slow, undulating mating dance, calling to his very core.

He breathed deeply, the scent of her filling his senses. Enticing, alluring, amazing. He tasted, just the smallest flick of his tongue.

Oh, God. Delicious. He was hit by an overwhelming wave of desire. So strong, if he'd been standing it would've knocked his feet right out from under him.

His tongue slid enticingly along her lips, then he pulled back just an inch and blew on the pouting flesh. She gasped. Needing to send her higher, he reached up with one hand to flick a berrylike nipple, its pink, puckered flesh hardening even more at his touch.

His eyes met hers again, his mouth still feasting, his finger dancing over her breast. Her eyes were midnight dark, passion pooling in her heavy-lidded gaze. There was a trust, almost innocent, in those eyes that tugged at Sebastian's heart.

But it was the sight of her body, spread out here for his questing pleasure, that drowned out any crazy emotional thoughts. He wanted her. He needed her. He was getting all he could get out of her. He had to.

Voracious now, he gave in to his insatiable hunger for her. His fingers worked, sending her higher as he tasted the evidence that she liked his technique. Her hips were moving faster, pressing, circling.

Her head fell back against the deck, so all he could see was the long line of her throat and the sharp jut of her chin. But he could see her pulse pounding, fast and furious, against that delicate white flesh.

Sebastian intensified his ministrations. His tongue swirled, then, fingers strumming her breasts like fine instruments, he sucked the heated nub between his teeth and gently nipped.

Jordan's gasp pierced the night.

Pleasure surged through him at the escalating sound of her panting moans. Her body clenched, legs tight against the sides of his neck, her thighs quivering. The moonlight shimmered beams of light over the pebbled perfection of her breasts, shaking with her rapid breaths.

As if it was his own climax, he felt the desperate driving need for release. She had to come. She was so close, right there on the edge. In that moment, the most important thing in his world was sending her over to the other side.

He kicked his efforts up another notch. Tongue, teeth and fingers all worked desperately, driving her higher. Faster.

Then it happened. Her back arched, her moans becoming a keening cry of exultation. Sebastian's groan joined hers as he slipped back a little, resting his cheek against the smooth, cool flesh of her inner thigh. His fingers downshifted from enticing to soothing, gently guiding her back down from that very gratifying pinnacle of pleasure.

He noted that his hand was shaking and was grateful that his ass was resting on the seat of the hot tub, otherwise he'd probably collapse.

God, had he ever experienced anything so incredible? So powerful?

So freaking emotional?

Sebastian closed his eyes and breathed in Jordan's musky

scent, forcing himself to concentrate on the feel of the hot water eddying around him. Counting backward from thirty, he finally leveled his own pulse and was able to take stock of his body.

Heart racing? Check.

Brow damp with sweat? Check.

Muscles clenched in anticipation? Check.

Dick limp as a wet noodle? Check, dammit.

But even as he uttered his now familiar curse, he couldn't find the anger to support it.

His eyes still closed, head resting against her thigh, he felt Jordan move. Her long, satisfied moan echoed over the water, filling his ego with pride. She stretched, slow and sinuous.

Then she almost killed him. With a soft purr, she rested a gentle hand on the side of his face. A whisper of a caress said more than all the words he'd ever written.

It said thank you. Beautiful. Wow.

All that, and more.

His heart, something he'd never been sure he had, swelled. Without conscious volition, he grinned, big and goofy, and pressed a kiss to her thigh.

Limp dick aside, damned if he didn't feel great.

Not that he was about to thank that witch who'd cursed him. But Sebastian could secretly admit that this had been, hands down, the most intense, powerful sexual encounter of his life.

Which was even more terrifying than the idea of his dick never manning up to do its damned job again.

6

DRIFTING IN THAT LOVELY place between sleep and waking, Jordan rolled over and wrapped her arms around her pillow with a sigh. God, she felt good. Satisfied. Then she groaned as the sunshine streaming through the bedroom window flashed an unsympathetic wakeup call against her closed eyelids.

Had it all been a dream?

Tugging a pillow over her face in protest, she stretched and yawned her way awake. Limber and deliciously hypersensitive, she was happy to note her body was still feeling the aftereffects of one very impressive orgasm.

Nope, no dream.

Mmm. She grinned, pulling the pillow off her face and cuddling it tight in her arms. Yeah. That had been the stuff legends are made of. Sexy, intense and just a smidge selfish. She shook her head in wonder. She, the personification of approval seeking, right down to her blow-job technique, had gloried in a mind-screaming climax.

All. By. Herself.

Pure heaven, then, suddenly it was over. Jordan sighed and stared at the ceiling, chastising herself for being ungrateful. But, she'd craved the feeling of his body in hers, of watching him explode with satisfaction. Instead, he'd given her the softest, sweetest kiss. He'd given her a hug and made a joke about rumors not giving him nearly as much credit as he deserved. Then he'd stepped out of the tub, wrapped his gorgeous body in a towel before she'd had even a second to appreciate the sight and offered his hand to help her out.

Who knew the Golden Boy stud was so unselfish? For the first time, Jordan had looked past his reputation to see the sweet man that he was.

And fallen just a little in love.

Scared, she tossed the pillow aside and rolled out of bed. A part of her wanted to hurry downstairs, wanting to see Sebastian again, to find out what he was doing. How he'd look at her. What he'd say.

If he'd be willing to offer up another orgasm along with breakfast.

She forced herself to head for the shower. As she washed her hair, though, she remembered the rest of the evening. How, after assisting her from the hot tub, he'd gently wrapped her in a towel. Then with one arm around her still-trembling shoulder, he'd walked her inside, to the foot of the staircase.

He'd pulled her close. Looked into her eyes, given her that sexy half smile of his, and kissed her on the nose.

Then, instead of taking her to bed for another round of body-shaking climaxes? He'd patted her ass and sent her upstairs.

Here, alone under the pounding spray of water, Jordan could admit the truth. If only to herself. For one brief second, she'd worried. She'd wondered. She'd even freaked out a little. Had she done it wrong? Too loud? Too quiet? Too...what? She didn't know any other way to come, for crying out loud.

And how ridiculous was it to worry about something like that? It wasn't as if he'd been rating her blow-job technique. A person couldn't orgasm wrong.

Which, she realized as she slowly soaped her body, might

be the problem. If she was always reeling in the losers, the total toads, maybe it wasn't them. Maybe it was her.

Not that she believed it was her. Not really. Just because a girl had a lousy dating track record and a rotten relationship with her father didn't mean she had issues with men.

Although she had to admit, her plan to have wild sex with a coworker for the weekend, with the intention to never do or mention it again once they left the mountain might be little questionable.

Twenty minutes later, Jordan descended the stairs again. This time, instead of a towel and scented lotion, she was wearing a pair of low-slung jeans and a sheer floral blouse. Totally feminine, a little edgy and definitely sexy. She wondered if Sebastian would like it.

As she reached the end of the hallway it hit her. The scent of potatoes frying in onions and maybe, she sniffed, a bit of garlic. Oh, baby. Whatever he was making smelled almost as delicious as Sebastian had made her feel the night before.

Pretending she wasn't shaking just a little in her jeans, she plastered a breezy smile on her face and stepped into the kitchen. She tried to ignore the nerves fluttering in her stomach as she wondered what he'd say. How he'd look at her. Whether he'd be willing to go another round before breakfast.

"Morning," Sebastian said, obviously hearing her entrance since he didn't turn away from the stove.

"Hey there," she replied, heading straight for the coffeepot. She skidded to a halt a foot away and squinted. Empty? How was that possible?

It was hard not to freak at the idea of having a conversation with the man whose mouth had made her see stars before she'd had her morning coffee. She filled the pot and added grounds. She pressed Start and watched the dark liquid fill her waiting cup, then switched it out with the coffeepot. After, taking a deep sip, she turned to smile at Sebastian.

Who wasn't paying her the slightest attention. She gave a deliberate hum of appreciation at the sight of the food he was cooking.

Nothing. He was still watching his frying pan as if the answer to all the world's ills would appear in the pattern of potatoes and onions.

Jordan frowned.

Maybe she had come wrong.

"How'd you sleep?" she asked. "Comfy?"

"Yeah, I slept great," he said, adding a few dashes of cayenne and paprika to the frying vegetables.

"Warm enough?"

He gave an odd little shudder, then nodded. "Yep, it was fine. Plenty comfortable."

Irritation splashed over the edges of her orgasm-induced morning cheer.

Jordan gave herself an entire two minutes. She drank the rest of her coffee. She refilled the cup. She leaned against the counter and counted to ten. Then she couldn't stand it anymore.

"So what's the problem?" she challenged. "I've seen you in the morning before, you're not anti-sunshine. So what is it? Are you one of those guys who get pissy if a woman initiates sex? Or are you just the bedpost-notching type and not getting your rocks off throws your count?"

As soon as the last word left her tongue, Jordan wanted to yank them all back. Oh, God, what was wrong with her mouth? This was so not the way to win friends and influence the guy to give her more mind-melting orgasms. And it made her sound more than a little bitchy.

But at least it got his attention. Shoulders braced for an angry confrontation, she watched Sebastian slowly tap the spatula on the side of the frying pan. Once, twice, then three times. She gulped, her hands trembling just a little on her coffee cup. Was he trying to keep himself from throwing it at her? She'd never seen evidence of a temper in him before, but maybe he was like her dad and just kept a charming lid on it at work?

Then he turned around. Eyes wide, she inspected his face. Her stomach settled when she saw the amusement in his eyes and that sexy half smile of his. Smiles were good.

Spatula still in hand, he crossed his arms over his chest. Tilting his head to one side, he gave her a smooth once-over. His eyes lingered on her breasts, their tips tightening erotically against the delicate lace of her purple bra. He raised a brow at her jeans, whether because of their tight fit or the strip of bare skin visible above the waistband, she couldn't tell.

From the heat warming his golden green eyes when they returned to hers, either way, he liked what he saw. Jordan pressed her lips together, remembering the look in those eyes last night as he'd watched her explode with passion. Desire, damp and needy, pooled at the juncture of her thighs.

"What's the matter?" he asked with a wicked grin. "Get up on the wrong side of the bed this morning?"

No. She'd got up alone this morning, but she wasn't about to tell him that.

"What's the matter with you?" she shot back. "You forget your manners this morning, or is this how you handle awkward morning afters?"

He snickered and shook his head. That's when Jordan saw it. The lines of stress and worry bracketing his eyes, creasing his forehead. The same lines she'd noted on Thursday at the editorial meeting.

"Look, sorry. I'm having a bad morning," he apologized.

His tone was light and friendly. "It has nothing to do with you. Or what happened last night."

The words were on the tip of her tongue. What was wrong? But she swallowed them.

What a chicken she was.

All she needed now were a few feathers to complete her wimp status. If she was interested enough in the guy to lure him into the hot tub with her naked body, she should damned well have the nerve to ask him personal questions.

Squaring her shoulders, Jordan did just that. "Are you okay? I know last night was—"

"Last night was great. I was working through a problem, totally spacing out," he interrupted before she could detail exactly what the night had been. Then he gestured with the spatula. "How about breakfast?"

Not sure if she was irritated or grateful, Jordan asked point blank, "Is the problem being stuck up here in the mountains with me?"

Something flashed across his face. She saw surprise, irritation and something else. Fear? She couldn't figure it out.

"See," Sebastian pointed out, "This is one of the reasons you run into problems at *Machismo.* You don't have enough confidence in yourself to wait out the competition. Instead you let irritation get the better of you and smart off. Or you jump to the wrong conclusions. Or both."

Warmth heated Jordan's cheeks. Well, that was an effective distraction, wasn't it?

"Are you saying we're competing?" she challenged, sidestepping the rest of his comments.

"Aren't we?" he gave her another long, searching look, then turned to stir his potatoes again. "These are done. Want to grab the juice? I figured we could eat on the patio."

No, she didn't want to grab the juice. She wanted to know what the hell he meant.

But, despite his accusation, she knew the value of timing. So she snagged the glass pitcher, grabbing the dish of toast on her way out the sliding glass door. Then she grinned. There on the small wooden porch she saw he'd set the table all pretty, complete with cloth napkins and a flower. He'd obviously got the plates, a brilliant turquoise, from the box she'd left on the back counter. She didn't have the heart to tell him she'd be breaking them to bits as soon as they were washed.

"Wow," she said, seeing that the food looked as good as it smelled. Along with the potatoes and toast, he'd made chive-and-cheese scrambled eggs and fried ham. Fat city, but she didn't care. She couldn't remember the last time a guy—hell, anyone outside of a restaurant chef—had cooked for her.

She wasn't going to let that stop her, though. She filled her plate first, then asked, "So if you know so much, what am I doing wrong?"

"I didn't say you were doing anything wrong."

"You're the one who said I had problems at *Machismo,*" she pointed out. "I get the crap assignments, fluff and filler. My ideas are only good if they are handed off to someone else. Half the staff acts like I've got cooties and the other half like I'm the golden goose."

"You do have a few challenges, don't you?" He considered, like he didn't want to rock the boat too much, then scooped up a forkful of aromatic potatoes before asking, "I don't get it. You're a good reporter. You could have your pick of your magazines to work at. Olliver Publications or any other place. Why *Machismo?*"

Jordan shrugged and started to toss off a glib excuse, then she saw the look in his eyes. Concern. Real, heartfelt concern.

She sighed, a corner of her heart melting into a puddle. Just one corner, though, she assured herself.

"I want…no, need to prove something. To my father, to myself," she admitted. "As far back as I remember, Daddy's wanted someone to hand the business down to. I want to be that someone. Oh, not because of the money. All of us girls are financially set. Because I wanted to prove I was as good as any son. That I have what it takes to work my way up. From the bottom up."

"Editorial?"

"Eventually," she nodded. "I like reporting. But I like the ideas more, coming up with concepts and story proposals. Like the column. That excites me more than going out scoping for news."

"You're good at it," he agreed. Then he grinned. "At least, you are when you keep the audience in mind."

Jordan smirked.

"And you think you can handle that?" he asked in a serious, contemplative tone.

She shrugged, stabbing a forkful of potatoes and eggs with a frown. It sounded so lofty and conceited, didn't it? Maybe she could convince him she'd just been kidding?

"Hey, I'm not doubting you, I'm just clarifying. I didn't realize that's the direction you were interested in." He reached over and nudged her chin so she'd look at him. His eyes were warm, with no hint of derision or amusement.

"You're the first person I've told," she admitted.

Jordan didn't know what the feelings were tumbling around in her stomach. Nerves, definitely. Hope, a little bit of irritation. But there was something else. A soft, trembling sort of emotion. If she didn't know better, she'd be scared. Because it felt as if she was falling in love.

"I think you'll be incredible. I know I'd work under you."

He gave her a naughty grin, then continued, "If I can help, put in a good word, I'll be happy to. Whatever you need, count me in, okay?"

"I thought..." she hesitated.

"Thought that's the direction I wanted to go?" he asked.

"Yeah."

"Nah. I like the unpredictability of reporting." His grin was pure charm, but she saw the stress and hurt in his eyes. Sure, he might like reporting, but he was ambitious. And he'd willingly step aside, let opportunities pass.

For her.

Jordan frowned as a flash of light sparked bright. Probably the sun coming through the clouds, glinting back off the window, she told herself. She was sure it wasn't the tears she had to blink fast to hide.

Well, hell. Looked like she really had just fallen in love.

SEBASTIAN SQUINTED, almost blinded by the explosion of light. Damn, wasn't a limp dick and freckles enough? Did he have to have vision issues, too?

"You okay?" he asked, his eyes adjusting so he could see her face again. She was pale and a little stunned looking.

"Um, yeah." She looked down at her plate, took a breath, then shrugged. "I'm good. I think. But I'm curious. You said you're willing to help me out. How about some advice? You see how things go down at *Machismo*. How do I change that?"

Preferring to talk business to whatever it was that'd put that fragile look in her gorgeous eyes, Sebastian took a second to gather his thoughts.

"Quit worrying so much," he finally suggested.

"I beg your pardon?"

"You worry. You obsess. You are always trying to make

people happy at the expense of what you want. Take that article last week, the Valentine's thing. You wanted to slant it one way, Garret another. You gave in instead of compromising."

"Easy for you to say," she said, giving him the most adorable little nose-scrunch before she scooped up more scrambled eggs. "You write with the advertisers in mind. You snag all the top stories, whether you come up with them yourself or not. Don't try and tell me you're not about making the suits happy."

All he could do was grin. Was there anything sexier than a woman with brains, attitude and a mouth made to deliver snappy put-downs. That mouth, it drove him crazy. One look at it and all he could think of was sex. The rich scent of her coffee reminded him of the sacrifices he'd made the last couple weeks trying to get his performance issues fixed. More exercise, less TV. No caffeine, more oysters. Hell, he'd even given in to humiliation and visited the doctor for a stash of those useless little blue pills.

Which meant that Jordan and her sassy mouth needed to stay off limits. Focus, he reminded himself. If he couldn't give her his best time, he could at least give her good advice.

"You don't have to stop slanting things in a way that people can get behind," he told her. "You just have to quit putting their desires before your own wants and needs. You want the article to inform men how idiotic scratchy lace lingerie is, talk up the benefits of silk. There's always a way to make your point and still make the powers-that-be happy."

She started to speak, then stopped. He was sure she was going to make a smart-ass comment, but instead she gave him a long, considering look then nodded.

Always tops when it came to gauging whether his subject

was ready to divulge more information or needed to regroup, Sebastian didn't push it. After a few minutes of silence only broken by the sound of utensils hitting china, Jordan pushed her gratifyingly empty plate away.

"Not that I'm saying I agree with your interesting—" she stopped, as if searching for the least offensive words "—assessment of the situation. But you have to admit, this sudden urge to offer up career advice is a little out of character. Especially when that advice is in direct conflict with your own career goals."

"It took the rest of your breakfast to come up with that polite way to say you think I'm full of shit?" he asked with a grin, before he tucked away the last bite of his toast.

Her lips twitched, but she kept the smile from surfacing. "You don't give me enough credit," she taunted. "I came up with that in seconds. But I wanted to do the food justice, so I waited."

Sebastian burst into laughter. She didn't give an inch. As incredible as it'd been nibbling his way over her body, feeling her explode and enjoying the feel of her body convulsing around his fingers, he wanted to be inside her. To feel her slick folds tighten around him, milking every blessed ounce of pleasure he knew he'd have with her body.

Fury flashed through him, just for a second, at the curse.

But, no. Instead of being pissed, he should be grateful. If not for the curse, he'd be doing Jordan on the table right this second. He wouldn't be able to resist.

And she deserved better.

7

"HEY, DON'T LOOK ALL grumpy like that," Jordan joked, laying her hand over his. It was all he could do not to turn his so they were palm to palm. When he met her eyes, she gave him a teasing little smile. "You'll end up looking like my father. You know, all uptight and frowny."

Sebastian laughed. He couldn't help it. "Frowny?"

"That's what my sisters call it. He gets this look—his brow sort of creases into his chin—whenever he doesn't want to talk about something. You know, things like dreams, troubles, the future. My mom, anything emotional like that."

Sebastian couldn't help it. At the flash of sadness in her eyes at the mention of her mom, who he knew had died when she was a toddler, he did turn his hand. Palm to palm, he meshed his fingers with hers and gave a squeeze.

"That must make it hard to communicate about your career goals then," Sebastian pointed out.

"It all depends on what you mean by communicate. If you're referring to the sessions where I pour out my plans and goals and he ignores me, we communicate just fine. Or the other ones. You know, where he lectures and lays out all the reasons I'm failing to meet his requirements for a well-behaved daughter?"

Sebastian bit off an angry growl. It wasn't just her words; the casual acceptance that it wouldn't change infuriated him.

She just shook her head and winked like it didn't matter. "Your name comes up a lot in those particular lectures. He thinks you're all that and a box of chocolates."

He shook his head. "Quit giving in to that game, then," he told her. "You're good at what you do, Jordan. You've got a dream and a plan to make that dream happen. Why are you letting your father ruin it for you? Just stand up to him, for God's sake."

She rolled her eyes. "Yeah, right. You know how parents are."

He dismissed that with a shrug. "Not really. Even controlling ones are better than what I had."

And didn't that sound melodramatic? Sebastian winced, forcing himself not to slump into his chair. This was the reason he never shared. It was impossible to even say the words aloud without sounding like a movie-of-the-week reject.

When Jordan gave him a questioning look, he did shift.

"What do you mean?" she asked quietly.

For some reason, he couldn't lie or evade. Not with her. So he said it fast, like ripping off a bandage.

"I don't know who my father was. He took off before I was born." He saw the sympathy flash in those caramel eyes and continued quickly, before she could say anything. "Christie, my mother, was a part-time phone operator, full-time alcoholic. I grew up on the streets of L.A., ran wild until I watched one of my buddies gunned down in a random drive-by. I decided then and there to get the hell out. To make something of myself. I've been working at it ever since."

Horrified, her eyes filled with tears.

"I didn't tell you that for sympathy," he snapped. Hell, he had no idea why he'd told her. Nobody knew, including Olliver. Although if he did, the old man would probably give up his Sebastian-for-son-in-law campaign. "The past is the past. I meant what I said, though. Just because things have always been a certain way, your dad being overbearing for instance, doesn't mean they have to stay that way. You have choices, Jordan."

Sebastian clamped his mouth shut, irritated that he'd offered up such an arrogant lecture. Who was he to tell her what to do? He waited for her justified retaliation.

Instead of tearing into him, though, she narrowed her eyes and gave him a long, considering look.

"You know, you might want to see a dermatologist," she suggested, totally changing the subject.

"Huh?"

"You've always had pretty decent skin."

Sebastian's brain couldn't find the connection. He was talking ideas and trust and she was talking skin care? Then he realized she was making it easy for him. Changing the subject so he didn't feel uncomfortable. What a sweetheart.

He gave her a slow, charming smile. His ego swelled. She'd noticed his skin. She really did have a thing for him.

Apparently his ego came through loud and clear, even without words. Jordan's own skin grew a shade pinker, but she jutted out her chin stubbornly and shrugged.

"Just saying, last week I noticed you'd suddenly broken out in freckles. Now they're fading. It's winter and you haven't been vacationing in a sunny locale. So, like I said, you might want to see a dermatologist. With come-and-go freckles, you're probably getting some weird skin condition and will have to quit your job and leave the field wide open for me anyway."

So much for having a thing for him.

She laid a friendly hand on his knee. An arrow of excitement shot through Sebastian at her touch, innocent though it was. Then, as if realizing she'd initiated the first physical contact since he'd had her naked, she pulled back and bit her lip. She stood, clearing the long-finished breakfast dishes as if nothing had happened.

"Look," she said quickly, not meeting his eyes. He didn't know if it was his confession or his nagging her to stand up for herself that had got to her, but he could tell she wanted some space. "I've got some things to do. I'll catch up with you in an hour or so, okay?"

Then she gave him a smile. It was like a shy ray of sunshine peeking from behind the clouds. Small, hopeful and sweet.

He felt it all the way to his heart.

Calling himself a sap, Sebastian left the table without another word. He headed outside and followed the now well-trodden path through the woods. Five minutes later, he strode along the bank of the lake, kicking at the stones in his way and wishing like crazy he could get the hell out of here.

He reached a familiar round, waist-high boulder. His perch last night. After going crazy with Jordan, he'd run. Like a total sissy. The first time in his life he'd had something he wanted, so much he'd almost gone mad wanting, and he'd had to walk away.

As he had the night before, Sebastian vaulted himself to the rock and sat, staring out over the lake and wondering. Did walking away make him a loser? Or the strongest man on earth? A guy who obsessively guarded his secrets to success, he'd just handed over a half dozen prime ideas to the woman who readily declared herself his competition.

He briefly considered contacting some editors at a few other magazines he knew. Olliver's influence was strong, but so was Sebastian's. He could call in a few favors, maybe find one or two publications that'd be willing to risk the old man's ire and give Jordan the shot she rightfully deserved.

Not quite the same as giving her the incredible sexual adventure he'd dreamed of for so long, but it was apparently all he had to offer.

Sebastian sat, a feeling of righteous nobility wrapping around him like a cloak. Hey, even if he wasn't getting what he wanted, at least he was doing the right thing.

Then he reached down and picked up a fat rock. And with an animal growl of fury, he heaved the rock into the lake with all the pent-up frustration and hurt ripping through his gut.

JORDAN PACED THE LENGTH of the deck. Back, forth and back again. The French doors stood open, a four-foot frame set up on the worktable and a couple dozen tins of broken china on the counter.

But she couldn't concentrate. She couldn't create. Hell, she couldn't even stay still.

All she could do was replay Sebastian's words. Over and over and over. He was right. She never pushed for what she wanted. Sure, she set goals and worked toward them. But the first hard wall? She gave up and settled right there, at the base of the wall, like it was her new home.

Hell, even while Sebastian gave her that peek into his past, into his heart, she'd wanted to push. To empathize and tell him what an amazing man he'd made of himself. But he'd slammed up a boundary and she'd clamped her mouth shut, then took the easy route by changing the subject to his damned freckles. Freckles, for crying out loud!

All these years, she'd accepted the very simple principle that she couldn't have everything she wanted. She'd never be tall, she couldn't pull off blond and her father's respect came with a price tag.

And while she'd gotten used to wearing heels, and come

to appreciate her own natural auburn hue, she'd never been able to wrap her mind around the concept of giving up the fight for Daddy's respect.

But what if Sebastian was right? What if she could have a little piece of her own dream and prove herself to her father?

Wasn't it worth a shot?

Before she could stop herself, Jordan strode into the kitchen and grabbed the phone. She punched zero and waited.

"Daddy? I need a minute."

"A minute is all I can spare."

She didn't waste a second wishing for anything more. Instead, she dove into her pitch. Her words, fast and excited, tumbled out. "I want the column. I want you to back me on it, too. I've got a great idea to not only make it sing, but to bring in a whole new advertising sector."

"Oh, please, Jordan Marie. Do we have to waste time with this?"

"It's not a waste." She took a deep breath, then risked it all. "You saw my column suggestion. It's good. It shows a solid feel for the readership, the advertisers. But it still has an edge. It doesn't cater, it engages. Give me a chance."

She hadn't finished uttering the last syllable when he snorted. Deflated before he even started talking, Jordan sank to the stool and tried to keep the tears at bay.

"Ridiculous," he dismissed. "This has gone on long enough, young lady. Quit playing at the magazine. Get a suitable job. It was bad enough you wasted your years at college getting a degree in journalism. You're a girl, Jordan. Start acting like one."

"My being female has nothing to do with my job qualifications," she insisted as her stomach churned. "I'm a damned good reporter. Or I would be if you'd stop stonewalling me."

"Quit making as if you're one of the big boys. You're way out of your league."

Unable to even find the words through the anger pounding in her head, Jordan gave a low, strangled scream.

Too furious to even hang it up, she threw the phone across the room. The loud clatter as it and its battery separated gave her no satisfaction.

Frantic, clueless what to do next, her gaze landed on her computer bag there on the breakfast bar. Tears blurred her vision as she stared at her laptop, the urge to e-mail her resignation overwhelming.

Knowing she had to do it, Jordan flipped the laptop open, booted up a blank document and started typing.

As if the discussion with Sebastian had opened a painfully guarded floodgate, she couldn't stop the words from flying over the screen. Everything she was, everything she'd been so long denied, came pouring out.

Thirty minutes later, she hit send.

And stared, empty of all emotion, as the confirmation flashed across the screen.

Her mind blank, she pushed away from the counter and went into the workroom. She looked at the colors she'd chosen, all bright and pretty. Then she turned around and headed for the china cabinet in the formal dining room.

With an evil grin, she pulled out the padded china cases holding the black porcelain plates her father loved so much and lugged them to the workroom and waiting hammer.

She'd just started on the gravy boat—who the hell wanted gravy out of a tacky black vessel with gold swirls anyway—when she heard the door close.

Hammer resting on her shoulder, she stormed into the kitchen to lay into Sebastian for his idiotic idea.

And damn near dropped the hammer on her foot.

"What happened to you?" she asked, staring.

He looked as if someone had tried to drown him. Other than his bare feet, he was still fully clothed in the same T-shirt and jeans he'd worn at breakfast.

Except now his clothes were dripping dank lake water all over the tile floor. His hair, usually so sexily tousled, hung in streaming strings down his neck and across one eye. And even from ten feet away, she could see the goose bumps coating his arms.

"Did you fall in?" she asked, rushing over to the laundry room to grab a stack of clean towels.

Hurrying back to him, she grabbed one and dropped the rest on the chair. With a flick of her wrists, she had it unfolded and wrapped around his shoulders. Then, standing on tiptoe, she started rubbing it over his sopping hair.

"I went for a swim," he muttered, not meeting her eyes.

"Swim?" She dropped the ends of the towel and stepped back. "It's January. The lake is like ice."

"No shit."

"So you just, what? Jumped in? Are you crazy?"

Now his eyes were on hers, hot anger flaming in the golden depths. "I wanted to swim," he bit off.

"I guess this is what you mean about not letting anything, even intelligence, get in the way of doing what you want," she snapped, furious that he'd take such a risk with his health. At least, that was part of her fury. The rest, she hated to admit, was because of his stupid damned advice. He'd pushed her. Encouraged her. Nagged her into confronting her father.

Now everything had changed. And there was no way it'd ever go back to what it'd been. Even if what it'd been had totally sucked.

Terror clutching her belly at the prospect propelled her two steps forward. She stood so close he dripped water on her floral blouse. She glared up into his face and demanded, "You're so good at pleasing yourself, aren't you, Sebastian? Because you're the only person you care about. All by yourself there, you don't have to give two good damns about anyone else in your world, do you?"

His face was a study in frustration. Anger, helplessness and mourning flashed through his eyes, then his expression settled into those superior lines of disdain she hated so much.

Jordan would give anything to be able to pull off such a supremely arrogant look.

"If you want to succeed, you don't wait for things to fall into your lap. You go out and grab them."

Obviously arrogance was overrated.

But the attitude behind his words did do one thing. It blew to pieces any hesitation or timidity she had left.

"You think you're so smart? You think I should just grab what I want and by grabbing, I'll get it? Get to have it? To use it? To, what? Even keep it?"

His just stared.

"You're wrong."

And to prove it, Jordan did the one thing she'd been wanting to do since last night. For the past two years, even. She stepped away from him, just a few inches so she had room to maneuver. She unsnapped her low-cut jeans and with a quick shove, she dropped them to the floor. He backed away, shaking his head in denial.

But the look in his eyes didn't say no. That look said "Oh, yeah, baby. Please and fast."

It was for that look that she stripped off her frothy top and stood there, clad in only her purple lace bra and panties and slapped her hands on her hips.

"Go for what I want? Not give up?" she mocked. "Fine, then. What I want right now is for you to quit dripping all over my floor. Strip."

"Look, Jordan," he protested, a layer of panic coating his words. "I can't make love with you."

Her heart spasmed, the pain sharp and intense. God, what was it with the men in her life?

"Just ask, hmm," she said, her sarcasm bouncing off his chest. "Sure, that works just fine. If people already want you. But when you're always rebuffed? The one who isn't good enough? The one who isn't wanted enough? Asking just adds that fun layer of humiliation to the rejection. Yep, that's great advice."

"You don't understand."

She threw up her arms and growled at him. "Understand? What's to understand? You're great at the pithy advice, but you don't want me. Simple enough."

Her words were clipped, dismissive. She knew they didn't show the pain and humiliation churning in her gut. That she could glare at him made her proud, since all she felt like doing was curling up in the corner and bawling.

But she was already naked enough.

"Jordan…"

"Isn't that princess?"

"Jordan, listen…"

For five long, breathless seconds, she waited. She didn't want to. She wanted to storm from the room in a fit of righteous indignation. But she couldn't. Dammit, she was so idiotically in love with the guy, all she could do was stand there and wait.

And stew in the terror that sudden realization evoked. It was all Jordan could do to keep breathing. In love. Oh, God, she was insane.

Then, slowly, reluctantly, like he was being forced at gunpoint, he reached down and tugged the hem of his shirt, lifting the sodden fabric over his head.

"What—"

"Look," he interrupted, his words slow and forced, as if he was about to confess that he'd gotten soaked burying his last lover at the bottom of the lake. "You need to know something. You deserve the truth."

His hands went to the snap of his jeans, tugging hard on the wet, uncooperative fabric. Her eyes huge, she tried to hide her lusty reaction. But, man oh man, he was just one delicious specimen of male perfection.

"What truth?" she asked, pretending she cared what he said. But given the choice between words and action, all her body wanted was to see his, naked.

"I…can't."

His jeans hit the floor with a loud, wet thud. His dick strained impressively against his blue pinstriped boxers. Jordan licked her lips, her heart beating fast enough to drown out half his words.

"Can't, what?"

He hesitated, pain etched on his face. He closed his eyes, as if gathering strength, then confessed.

"Can't make love to you."

8

Torn between his words and the sight of his now naked and very turned on body, Jordan didn't know whether to throw something at him or jump him.

"Right, because that—" she gestured to his very hard, impressively large dick, standing at attention against the light dusting of fur on his belly "—is what? Off limits?"

"It won't work," he said, moving toward her slowly, surely. For a guy who claimed he couldn't use his rock-hard tool, he was sure stalking her as if he could. The look of intent passion on his face made Jordan swallow to wet her suddenly dry throat. Maybe she really was out of her league.

"It worked fine last night," she argued, forcing herself not to back away as he loomed over her.

"Did it?" he asked, reaching out and sliding his fingers through her hair. He cupped the back of her head, pulling her inexorably closer. Then he moved, his icy-cold body pressing against hers. Jordan wanted to protest. To tell him to wait until she'd figured out what he was talking about. Or to at least come upstairs with her.

But the look on his face. Passion mingled with intense anger, held her mute. She stared up into his golden green eyes and, even though she felt completely safe, admitted to herself that he scared the hell out of her.

"You felt good last night?" he asked, bending down to brush his lips, so soft and tempting, over hers.

"I did," she whispered, risking her third rejection of the day by slipping her tongue along the soft cushion of his lower lip.

No rejection here, though. Instead, Sebastian groaned and took her hand, placing it on the velvety-hard length of his shaft.

Mmm. Jordan stroked her hand up, down, letting the rhythm build in layers. Like the ones inside her, flaming, heating, intensifying. Apparently unable to help himself, Sebastian pulled her mouth to his with a sexy little growl and kissed her as if he was a desperate man and she his only salvation.

The kiss, like the slide of her hand, built in layers. Sweet at first, with just a hint of sexual intention. Then it got hotter. His tongue moved over hers faster. Swirls became thrusts. Movements sped up, wilder, harder.

Jordan's breath came in pants now, her body tingling with awareness and need. A warm, aching dampness throbbed between her thighs. Whether he sensed it or whether it was the almost-begging movements of her hips against his thigh that got his attention, Sebastian reached down and cupped his hand over her damp panties.

Jordan's heart shuddered at his touch. His fingers pressed through the cloth, working her swollen nub into a state of high-pressured delight.

"You felt good last night," he repeated when she'd started climbing that delicious ladder of delight, making it a statement this time. "But me?"

Jordan didn't have to shake the sexual fog off her brain, it dropped away by itself at his question.

But him. She'd known it. Damn, he hadn't been Sir Gallant out of some unselfish gentlemanly focus on her pleasure. Jordan's body, so hot just seconds ago, went ice cold.

"You don't want me," she stated. Pain slashed through her. Even though she'd expected it, the rejection still ripped at her heart. She tried to step back, but he wouldn't release her. Before she could pull her hand away, he covered it, pressing her fingers tighter to the broad hardness of his quite impressive cock.

"Want is such an easy thing," Sebastian mused softly as his fingers slid under the elastic of her panties to slide over damp flesh, whisper soft and wildly enticing.

"Wants can be ignored," he continued, his other hand sliding up her side, tracing a heated path over her waist to the swell of her breast encased in purple lace. "Set aside."

His finger traced her aching nipple through the fabric, then flicked it once. Twice. Jordan barely stopped herself from mewling out a begging entreaty that he quit teasing and take her.

"You're right," he said as his mouth skimmed over her jaw, then down her throat, making her melt. "I don't want you."

As the words echoed in her head, he scraped his teeth over the rigid tip of her breast through the lace. Her hand still wrapped around the rigid steel of his erection, Jordan felt the passion radiating off his flesh. Like a screaming alarm, his body cried out unquestionably just how much he wanted her.

"Liar," she said as she gasped for air, barely able to hold on to the thread of conversation. Her mind spun, her heart raced.

"No," he insisted, lifting his head from her breast to look into her eyes. His gaze was like a laser, intense, fixed and deadly. "I don't want you, Jordan."

Even as he said the words, his fingers slid into her, one, then two. Gliding in, then out. Twisting to tease, to torment, to take her higher.

Before she could cuss at him for driving her crazy while he spewed lying words of rejection, he lowered his mouth to hers. Tongues tangled and danced, each of them vying for control. Lips meshed, a perfect fit. Her heart sped, her pulse pounded as she tilted there, just on the edge of an orgasm.

He slipped away, just his mouth and just a hairsbreadth back. Enough so he could look into her eyes as his fingers wove their magic.

"I don't just want you, Jordan. I need you. Need you like I've never needed anyone, anything in my life."

Jordan fell over orgasm's edge into wicked, mind-bending delight. Her body arched, her breath shuddered as she gave a keening cry of satisfaction. Her heart pounded in her ears, but she still heard, maybe felt, Sebastian's groan of delighted male ego. The sound sent an after-tremor through her, as if knowing he was glad he'd made her come made her want to do it all over again.

Jordan took her time, letting her breath steady, her heart settle. Sebastian needed her. Her. A grin, part satisfaction, part confidence, spread across her face.

"Sweetheart, does that feel like I don't want you?" he asked as he buried his face in the damp curve of her neck.

Jordan dropped her head to his now warm chest and watched her fingers, pale and delicate, move over his length. Then with a confused growl, she shifted her head to look at him.

"Explain," she demanded.

"I had an…Encounter." He said it as if he was confessing he'd had sex with a goat on national television. The horror and shame in his voice were echoed in his eyes. "The gal claimed to be a witch. I, misguidedly, laughed at her beliefs. So she cursed me."

Of all the stories she might have imagined, that one was nowhere on the list. Curses? Jordan couldn't laugh at him, not with him sporting that serious, hound-dog-that's-been-kicked look in his eyes. But she had to ask, "Um, cursed you how?"

"Let's just say things get a little, ah, flimsy when push comes to shove."

Jordan's lips twitched. Even Sebastian looked amused, a glint of laughter shining in his eyes when he saw she wasn't going to tear into him.

There was nothing flimsy about the hard, throbbing flesh under her fingers. Jordan was torn between the desire to find that bitch and tear her hair out and pull Sebastian close to comfort him for the obvious emotional stress he'd been under.

And for being a gullible—if adorable—sucker.

"You know, the power of suggestion can be a wicked influence." She caught the look on his face and stopped right there. Oops, bumping up against the naked male ego with a cattle prod probably wasn't smart.

"Are you saying it's all in my head?"

The jokes danced through her brain at the speed of light, but given that she had her hand full and didn't want to let go, she just shook her head.

"Of course not."

His chin jutted out almost as stiff as the flesh beneath her fingers. Jordan recognized that look. All her years of compromise came to the fore. Excitement curled in a tight coil in her belly. Not just at the idea of doing what she had in mind. But at the concept of her being the one to help him. Her, Little Ms. Nobody, rescuing the Golden Boy.

"Well, maybe, just maybe," she said in a soft teasing tone as she tiptoed the fingers of her free hand up his chest, "I can help."

"Look, Jordan—"

"You tried to help me, it's the least I can do for you," she said, leaning forward to press wet, openmouthed kisses to his chest. He shuddered, his dick swelling encouragingly.

She traced a gentle, teasing trail over the broad width of his shoulder then down to the tempting hardness of his biceps. Her body reacted in delicious wet enthusiasm to the hard feel of his muscles—all of them.

"But you said my help sucked," he said in a strangled tone.

"Turnabout is fair play, then, isn't it?" she teased, dropping to her knees in front of him. "I'll just have to make sure mine sucks, too."

His laugh cut off when her lips wrapped around the velvet head of his cock. He groaned, sinking his fingers into her hair as if he was holding on for dear life. More empowered than she'd ever felt before in her life, Jordan tossed aside all ideas of technique, what she should do, whether he'd like it or not, and just gave herself over to the movement.

Despite her fondling, his flesh was still chilly from his icy swim. Her lips slid, then sucked, alternating in a way that he obviously liked given his rapid breathing and how he was kneading his fingers in her hair.

He tasted so damned good. Jordan sucked, then with a gentle teasing motion, ran her teeth along the length of his glistening dick. He swelled appreciably.

God, she wondered, just how much bigger could he get. And how fun was it going to be to find out?

Wanting, needing, more, she pressed against his thighs. Ever the smart guy, Sebastian got the message instantly and dropped to the floor, lying back on the cool tiles and tugging on her hand to pull her up to him. Jordan shook her head.

"I'm not finished," she said with a saucy look. Jordan didn't plan to stop until she'd proved to Sebastian once and for all that there was no curse and that he was perfectly capable of giving her the incredible sex she wanted from him.

HE GRINNED AT JORDAN as she kneeled over him. He was torn between a groan and laughter at the wicked look of chastisement on her gorgeous face. Her lips were swollen and damp, proof that she'd been having quite a good time down south. Her breasts swayed in that sexy purple bra as she knelt between his outstretched legs. He needed to touch her. Wanted to feel her. Had to have her.

And then her lips were on him again. A lesser man would have cried in gratitude, it felt so damned good. She was so damned good. She pulled his dick deep into her mouth, the hot, wet suction making him clench his fists, raise his hips off the floor.

He couldn't remember feeling this good. Ever. Hell, in the last two weeks, he'd never lasted this long. The first hint of pleasure and wee willie winkie shriveled.

But this time? He was hard as a rock and still going strong. Was it Jordan? Was it the curse playing a cruel new trick, getting his hopes up only to dash them? Who cared, all that mattered was that he enjoy it as much as possible.

With that in mind, Sebastian grabbed her shoulders and tugged, pulling her up over him. Holding one hand behind her neck, he kissed her with all the pent-up passion and power he'd been missing.

Then he rolled. Her gasp echoed across the kitchen. He tugged, ripping her panties away. Too impatient to play nice, he shifted to his knees and grabbed her thighs, lifting her so her butt was a foot or so off the ground, her weight anchored at her shoulders.

"I'm sorry," he breathed, not sure if he was apologizing for his lack of finesse, his sucky foreplay or the desperate speed in which he was moving. Probably all of the above.

Then she smiled at him. A sensual stretch of her lips that said she was right there with him, any way, any speed he wanted to go. She ran her hands down his back, then, with a wicked grin, smacked his butt in a "let's rock" motion.

Her absolute confidence that he could rock, despite his confession, made Sebastian's dick harden even more. His body taut, his emotions as tight as a banjo string, he poised over her.

God, he didn't know what scared him more. That he'd plunge and find out he'd shriveled to nothing. Or that it'd work and he'd find out that Jordan really was the woman of his dreams.

Never one to avoid the truth, Sebastian held his breath, gathered her hands in his and stretched them up, over her head. Her breasts lifted, the full pillows pale and enticing against the vivid purple of her bra. He leaned down, tracing his tongue over the edge of the lace. Her moan of pleasure rang in his ears.

And he plunged. Dick rock hard, he drove himself into the heated warm welcome of Jordan's body. He could have cried, it felt so incredible.

Her body gripped his, squeezing as he thrust into her. She met every stroke with a twisting little shimmy. Sebastian's vision blurred, his brain shut off. He was pure sensation.

Oh, God, oh, God, oh, God. He silently chanted the prayer, and damned if it wasn't exactly that, as he pumped into the glorious wonder that was Jordan's body.

His chant setting the rhythm of his thrusts, his eyes locked with Jordan's, watching the passion flame and build in her dark gaze.

Sweat beaded his upper lip, his muscles quivered as he held himself steady, his arms locked, hands splayed across the tile floor. Even his shocked excitement over being able to do it, so to speak, wasn't enough to distract him from the incredible intensity building between him and Jordan. Looking into her eyes while driving thankfully into her body was the most intimate act he'd ever experienced.

Then her gaze clouded. Passion tightened her features as she sucked in her bottom lip.

Sebastian thrust harder. Faster. Her hips undulated, her breath came in mewling little gasps. He recognized the signs from last night. His moves grew more intense. He focused, with every fiber of his being, on bringing her over that sweet edge of pleasure.

Her breath came in faster. He trembled. Passion tightened to a painful pitch. Jordan's thighs gripped him, her body going taut as she arched up, nails digging into his shoulders. His vision went black around the edges, the power of his orgasm ripping through him like a tornado. With a guttural cry, Sebastian poured himself into her. His essence, his heart, his joy.

Then he collapsed, just aware enough to roll to the side as he dropped to the floor beside Jordan, wrapping one arm tight around her waist to keep her close.

"Well," she said a few minutes later after gulping in a few lungfuls of air, "I'd say you were wrong."

"Huh?"

"You most definitely could make love with me... and quite nicely, too."

She lifted her head from his chest to offer a naughty little smile. Satisfaction gave her an ethereal glow. It was almost magical.

And Sebastian, of all people, now recognized the true value of magic. And just how damned scary it really was.

He looked into her eyes, noting the easy humor and sweet contentment in those dark depths.

Like falling in love.

Crazy, but he knew it was true. And because it was, he trusted her. So he told her everything. Even about his unsuccessful attempts to cure himself.

He kept talking despite her snort of laughter over the spanking incident. Then he came to the part about today.

"So what are you saying?" she asked, a frown creasing her brow. "That because you, what? Trusted me? That's what it took to break the curse?"

Sebastian opened his mouth, then shut it. Despite his position on the floor, her body draped perfectly over his, he shrugged. He hadn't made that connection yet. Leave it to Jordan to see right to the heart of the situation.

"I see trust is a foreign concept to you," she teased.

"Not foreign. Just not one I'm overly familiar with." Then he gazed into her eyes. "I think it could grow on me, though."

Her smile touched his heart. Then she patted his face, and with a quick kiss, launched herself to her feet.

With a glance down at her body, naked but for her bra, color tinged her cheeks. But she just shrugged and said, "How about I find some clothes and meet you back here in ten minutes? I'm suddenly starving."

Before he could respond, she turned on her heel and practically skipped from the room. Sebastian grinned at the difference in her demeanor from what he was used to around the office. He'd love to credit it to his amazing sexual prowess, but even his ego couldn't condone that. After all, his prowess had consisted of not fizzling.

This time. Next round, he'd really give her something to skip about. But first, some dry clothes.

Sebastian was back in the kitchen within fifteen minutes, still buttoning his dry shirt. But Jordan wasn't there. She had, bless her heart, put on a pot of coffee. No longer worried about the effects of caffeine on his libido, Sebastian helped himself to a large cup. After all, with Jordan around he figured he'd never have a sexual problem again. Except for how hard it was going to be having to wait until he could make love with her again.

He'd finally found her. That mythical woman he could have fun with, talk seriously to, and most of all, trust. He'd had variations of the first two. But she was right, he'd never had the latter.

But Jordan? He'd trusted her with his biggest, darkest, most potentially humiliating secret. And what'd she done?

Broken his curse.

Just as he was contemplating which way and where he'd like that next fun encounter to happen, a loud chime got his attention. He glanced over and saw her laptop, open on the bar. Outlook was set to preview, so the e-mail was big and clear in size fourteen Lucinda.

He was snickering over Jordan's huge girly font when he noticed what the actual words said.

From Garret. About the column. His smile in place, he skimmed the first paragraph and damn near whooped aloud. She'd done it. She'd scored the column.

Sebastian didn't even feel a prick of regret as he happily kissed the income bump and challenge of a regular column goodbye. He was thrilled for Jordan, she deserved this. In so many ways.

Then his eyes dropped to the last paragraph.

"I didn't know you had it in you," it said. "When he finds out, he's going to be pissed. I hope you can handle the backlash. No second thoughts, though. I've already spread the word, so you're committed."

Spread the word? Sebastian's frown deepened. He who?

And pissed about what? Gossip? What, exactly, was the column she'd turned in?

Had she sold him out? Spilled his ugly secret? Gossiped about his past?

Mentally, Sebastian's entire world was crumbling. He ignored the misery that ripped through his belly at the idea of her selling him out.

He told himself he didn't care that his reputation as a lover might be shredded. In an ironic thanks to Jordan, he could easily disprove it. But if she went around telling people he thought he'd been cursed? He'd be finished as a journalist. His credibility would be shot and his gullibility a joke.

But this was Jordan. Why would she use him? How? Then he recalled the convenience of her appearance here at the cabin. And her lack of a vehicle to leave in.

Defenses honed on the streets and in the competitive magazine industry screamed a warning. Oh, yeah, she'd used him. Any doubts were erased when he remembered the gorgeous, body-stirring sight of her dropping that damned red towel.

"How about some homemade cinnamon rolls with that coffee," Jordan suggested in a cheery tone as she came into the room, her arms filled with a large sugar canister and a bag of pecans. "It'll take a couple hours for the dough to rise, but I'm betting we can find something to do while we wait."

She flashed him a teasing smile. If he didn't know better, he'd have said her heart was there, clear to see, in her eyes.

He thought of how sweet she'd been. Of how she'd listened, hadn't judged or mocked. How she'd taught him how to make love, how to break the curse. How to put a woman first.

He wanted to believe it was all true.

But he had an e-mail to prove that he actually didn't know jack.

9

"WHY DON'T WE TALK about that column of yours while we wait," Sebastian suggested.

Jordan pulled a face. She'd much rather get naked again. "What about the column? You have some advice to help me steal it out from under you?"

She shot him a teasing look, setting her cinnamon roll fixings on the counter. She opened a cabinet door and pulled out the commercial-grade food processor to start the dough, then glanced back at Sebastian.

He wasn't smiling. Actually, he wasn't looking anything like a guy who'd got lucky—both sexually and in terms of curse-breaking—on the very floor on which he was standing.

Nerves fluttered. Jordan shooed them away.

"What's up?" she asked. Then, unable to hold back her pitiful paranoia, she blurted out, "Did the sex not live up to your expectations?"

His eyes rounded, a flash of what might have been shame and worry lighting them before he shook his head.

"This has nothing to do with sex," he told her quietly, "and everything to do with your need for approval."

"I'd say I was more interested in your body than your approval," she joked. He just stared. The nerves settled, big and ugly, in her belly. "Okay, fine, why don't you tell me what the issue is here? What are you talking about?"

"I was just thinking. You've really done a lot to get your father's attention, haven't you?"

Not something she was thrilled about, but neither was she ashamed. It wasn't as if her father's attention was black market contraband. Jordan scanned his face, but couldn't figure out where this was headed. Needing to do something with her hands, she started measuring flour for the dough.

"In truth, I've been seeking his approval more than his attention," she said with a shrug, adding milk to the mixer and pushing Pulse while she melted butter in the microwave. "And only when it comes to my career. If I really wanted his attention, I'd have done something crazy a long time ago. Like date you."

She laughed and looked up from the mixer to share a wide, teasing grin. Only he wasn't smiling. Instead he was standing there, radiating judgmental attitude with an arrogant look on his face and his arms crossed over his chest.

"I asked you already, what's the problem?" she prodded. "Obviously something is. Does sex always make you this pissy?"

"Only when it's sex with a purpose."

"Purpose? Like what?"

"You used me," he snapped, his words fast and furious.

She had no idea what was going on. The nerves that'd settled in her stomach took on a sharp, edgy bite. Added to that, she was getting a little annoyed that he was so thoroughly ruining her happy sexual afterglow.

Obviously reason wasn't going to work with Sebastian, though. So she went for snark.

"Wasn't that a mutual using there on the floor?"

"You're trying to deny that you used me?" he challenged sarcastically.

"I categorically deny it," she shot back, hands fisted on her hips.

"Okay, sure. So suddenly, right after we…" He trailed off, his jaw clenching as if he was biting back ugly words. Then he shook his head and glared. "Just like that, you snagged the column?"

"After we what? Talked? Bumped uglies? How good do you think you are?" she asked. "Do you think I stole a little of your magical mojo or something?"

Then the rest of his words sank in. Jordan's anger dimmed as confusion washed through her. "I got the column? How would you know that?"

"Garret e-mailed."

"You?"

Sebastian winced. Then he just shrugged and gestured to her laptop.

"Your laptop was open."

She glanced over at the laptop in question on the dining room bar, then back at Sebastian. "You read my private e-mail?"

"You used me," he accused, skipping right over his own misdemeanor. "Was it all planned out, Jordan? Did your dad tell you he'd offered me the cabin this weekend, so you scurried up here to seduce me?"

Her jaw dropped. Her mind went blank. Jordan could only stare and replay his words, trying to figure out if he'd really said what she thought he'd said.

Then he continued, "Did you already call Daddy to fill him in on the details of our little encounter? Is that how you scored the column? Because he figured you'd finally started toeing the line? His reward for his little princess?"

Jordan hissed with anger. And she'd thought she could trust this guy? That he actually had emotional depth? She should have stopped at having her way with his body, since that's all there was to him.

"Oh, yeah," she shot back. "I totally used you. Just like you used me to break your curse, hmm?"

"What—"

"What'd you do, Lane? A little research and figure out that the curse would lift and you'd get possession of your dick back if you just made some gullible idiot fall for you?"

"That's not—"

"Or was this just a game for you? You made up that whole curse bullshit to see how far you could go. How much of a fool you could play me for."

"You're being ridiculous."

"Am I?" she snapped, finally losing her grip on both her temper and the pain ratcheting out from her heart and ripping her emotions to shreds. "I'm ridiculous?"

She shoved the food processor with all her strength, sending the heavy metal appliance to the floor with a huge crash and a cloud of flour.

"I've never used you, or anyone, Golden Boy. You think you're so damned hot, so damned special? Well for your information, the column proposal I sent in had nothing to do with you, Mr. Perfect, or your freaking awesome advice."

She stormed across the tile floor, kicking through the gooey flour on her way to the door.

"Jordan—"

She didn't slow down. She continued her rapid stomp out of the kitchen, only taking time to flip him off over her shoulder.

Five minutes later, goggles protecting her stinging eyes, she was smashing plates to smithereens.

IT WASN'T UNTIL she blinked the moisture from her eyes that she realized her fiestaware wasn't shards anymore. It was dust.

Jordan let out a scream of frustration and sent the ham-

mer flying. Oddly enough the sight of it, embedded satis-
factorily in the sheetrock on the other side of the room,
calmed her down.

Her father was gonna be so pissed that she'd messed up his
wall. Which was just another thing that proved Sebastian
wrong. She didn't use people to get Daddy's approval. Hell,
the last thing she wanted was her father approving of her love
life. If he did, that'd mean she'd sold out. Settled for one of
those warty frog clones he was always pushing off on her.

But after all those toads with their slack-lipped, sloppy
kisses, she'd finally found the one and only guy that she and
her father could agree on. Albeit for entirely different reasons.
And kissing him? He definitely wasn't a frog. But dammit,
that didn't make him a prince, either. Not after the things
he'd accused her of.

Jordan stomped across the room and tugged the hammer
from the wall. White dust swirled in the air as she freed it.

Using him, her ass.

She'd never use anyone to get her father's approval.

But, that naggingly honest little voice in the back of her
head reminded her, she had used him. For sex. To shore up
her confidence. To make her feel as if she was just as much a
woman as all the other gals he'd slept with.

Different motive, but it was using all the same.

Jordan almost threw the hammer back into the wall.

Instead, her chest constricting, she sank to the floor and
stared at the wood-and-steel tool. She'd used Sebastian. Just as
he'd said she had. What did that make her? Desperate? Pathetic?

Her head fell back against the wall and she stared out
through the French doors at the distant lake.

It made her, she finally admitted, a woman in love. She'd
always had a thing for Sebastian. Sure, she'd called it a crush,

tried to write it off as sexual curiosity. But it was, it had always been, unrequited love.

And, she cringed, considering how pissed he was at the idea that she'd used him, unrequited was the key word here.

Jordan sighed, wondering why she always picked the losing battles. She got to her feet, wincing a little at the pain in her still-bruised knee. Shoulders drooping, she crossed the room. It wasn't until she'd set the hammer on the pile of dish-dust that she realized what she was doing.

She was giving up. Just like that, a tiny obstacle and she was ready to call it quits. What a wimp. Sebastian had been right. So busy worrying that he thought she'd used him, she'd already given up.

She pulled her shoulders back and looked out at the lake again. Jaw clenched, she breathed deeply, then nodded and headed out the door.

If he was going to label her a user anyway, she might as well use his own advice to get him back. He'd said she gave up too easily, that she let the chip on her shoulder keep her from going after what she wanted.

Well not this time. What she wanted was Sebastian Lane.

And damned if she wasn't going to get him.

GOD, HE WAS AN ASS. A complete, unmitigated, braying jackass. He hadn't even had to cool off in the lake before he'd realized there was no way Jordan had sold him out.

Oh, not because she hadn't had time to e-mail his little confession to Garret. Although he'd realized that, too. No, she hadn't sold him out because Jordan didn't do that.

But he—so used to shoving people away from him, to keeping a nice safe distance from anything that might resemble trust—had jumped. Right to the wrong conclusion.

Just more evidence that she was too good for him. And he'd proven, as he'd known he would, that he was too much of a jerk for her.

Sebastian shifted and winced. His ass was planted on this damned rock once again and it was still uncomfortable as hell. Maybe the third time would be the charm, though, and he'd finally find some peace of mind here. Or at least escape Jordan, and seeing the pain he'd caused her, until the tow truck he'd called arrived.

Or not. He sensed rather than heard her making her way down the wooded path.

"Have you cooled off enough to talk yet?" she asked, stopping next to him.

"No."

"Okay, then. You can sit there brooding and listen. I'll do the talking."

Sebastian scowled. She'd always had a snarky mouth, but before her fear of rejection had kept her from pushing too far. Apparently that little issue was a thing of the past. He never should have given her that freaking pep talk.

"Look, princess, you and me, we're not the kind who can make it work." He ignored the hurt that filled her caramel eyes, pretending he wasn't feeling the same sharp, miserable pain. It didn't matter. Better to feel the sting now than give in to the hope that they could work.

"I've spent a lot of time dreaming about you. Wishing for you. But us in real life, though? That's a fairy tale, Jordan. We're from two different worlds. The princess and the L.A. street rat."

Jordan stared at him, sitting there on his rock all stoic and accepting. At least, he hoped he looked stoic and not pathetic like he felt.

"You know," she mused, "I always considered you the pinnacle of success. The Golden Boy, with everything you touch turning out perfect."

He snorted and shook his head. He couldn't blame her for the assessment. He'd spent his entire adult life fostering just that image. Yippee, it'd worked.

"Well now you know better," he said with a shrug.

"Yes, indeed. I do." She reached down and plucked one hardy golden bloom from the base of the rock. Sebastian didn't know if it was a weed or a flower, just that it was pretty.

Jordan twirled it between her fingers, then with an inscrutable look, handed it to him.

"What's this for?"

"You were right," she said.

"I usually am."

She rolled her eyes, then nudged him to scoot over so she could join him on the rock. Sebastian frowned. She obviously didn't have the woman-scorned demeanor figured out. But he moved anyway.

"Not right about me using you for the column. I read his e-mail. Garret was referring to my father as the person who'd be pissed. I did the unthinkable. I told my father I didn't want special favors, but that I was sick of being penalized for being his daughter."

"How'd that go over?"

"He told me if I couldn't handle it, I was free to quit."

Sebastian winced.

Before he could decide between cussing or condolences, she gave him a wicked little grin. The kind that made him very grateful the curse was lifted.

"I told him I could not only handle it, I'd handle it all the way to his competition."

"You didn't."

"I did," she laughed. "I even sent an email to a gal I met last year at Conde Nast."

Sebastian's jaw dropped. "You blackmailed him?"

Jordan tilted her head with a considering frown, then gave a rueful nod. "Yeah, I guess I did." Then her eyes rounded and she gave him a worried look. "I didn't get the column because of that, though. I checked. Garret swore he'd planned to go over my father's head on this anyway, that he loved my proposal that much."

He was nodding before she'd even finished the last sentence. "I know. He wouldn't have given it to you, and you wouldn't have taken it unless it was all legit."

Finally, he'd figured out that some people just didn't use others. The sweet, grateful look on Jordan's face filled him with joy.

Then she looked away. "You were right," she said softly. She didn't look at him, instead contemplating the lake. "You said I'd been hurt. That I was afraid to try but too stubborn to give up. You were right about that."

Then she leaned over and brushed a soft, sweet kiss on his cheek.

"What's that—" he gestured with the flower "—and this for?"

"You're just as hurt as I am. Who knew?"

Red alert. Definitely not a door she—or anyone—was allowed to go through. All defenses in place, Sebastian gave her his patented look of amused scorn.

"You're the one always trying to get your daddy's approval," he pointed out, not proud of stooping so low.

"And you're the one always trying to get everyone else's approval. Top reporter, best journalist. You're always shooting for number one." She ran her tongue over her bottom lip. Sebastian's dick stirred in interest. "That's why the curse had to be so rough on you. Your reputation is vital, the admiration of your legion of lovers essential for you."

"I'm not a horndog who only cares about sex," he defended.

"Oh, I know," she said quickly. Then she gave him a shy sort of look and admitted, "But you were right. I really did use you. Well, if you call seduction using."

"You're admitting it? After all that ugly crap I spouted, you're equating seducing me to using me?"

"The truth is almost as important to you as your reputation," she said with a shrug that told him she just thought she was stating the obvious.

Instead of blowing his mind.

He stared, stunned to his very core. Not once in his entire life had anyone ever understood him, accepted him, like Jordan did.

"You're the most amazing woman," he said slowly. Her eyes went wide as he took her hand and raised it to his lips. He brushed a kiss over the tender flesh of her palm and smiled. "You're stronger than you ever give yourself credit for. Smarter than anyone I know. You're savvy, snarky and sexy as hell."

A soft wash of color stained her cheeks as she smiled.

"I love you," he said quietly.

Her hand shook in his. This time he knew she'd heard him right. Her eyes filled with tears, but the smile on her face was pure joy.

"Really?" she asked.

"Really, really."

"I love you, too."

He hadn't realized how worried he was about her response. Tension fled, happiness taking its place. He pulled her tight, unable to find words to express how incredible he felt. So he showed her instead.

Finally, she broke away from his kiss to look into his eyes, as if assuring herself he'd spoken the truth. Her smile slowly grew, then rivaled the sun for brightness. She threw her arms around his neck and pulled him close.

"You never did tell me what your column proposal was," he said, wanting to hear her brag a little. Although he really didn't care what the topic was that'd beaten him out. Because he sure as hell didn't feel like a man defeated.

"Um, maybe we should talk about it later," she said quickly, as if she was afraid of denting his ego. Sebastian could have told her, though, that between her welcoming him back to sexual nirvana and her actually accepting—and loving—him despite his myriad of issues, his ego was unassailable.

"What'd you go with?" he prodded.

She pulled back a little and gave him a nervous little smile, then shrugged.

"I went with a humorous take on guys comparing dick size," she said, the words coming out in a rush.

Ouch. Maybe not so unassailable. Sebastian winced with his entire body.

"Along the lines of that competitive thing guys do. Always trying to keep up with the Joneses. Comparing sizes, cars, chicks and never seeing the upside to what you've already got," she said, her voice ringing with the same enthusiasm that lit her face. "I called it Nothing To Prove."

"Nothing To Prove?" he asked, a grin quirking as he imagined her father's reaction to not only her excellent idea, but that column title. The old guy would probably have a heart attack. "I like that. It's got a catchy ring to it and has un-limited topic potential."

"Exactly," she said. "Which you might want to keep in mind if you get the notion to go start trying to prove to yourself that the curse is lifted with any other women."

Sebastian's laughter rang out over the lake. He was still chuckling when Jordan pulled his face closer for a long, delicious kiss. As he tugged her down to the soft sand beside the rock, he realized she was right. He didn't have a single thing left to prove.

After all, he had Jordan. And what she brought to his life was pure magic.

* * * * *

"AREN'T YOU GOING TO SAY 'Fly me' or at least 'Welcome Aboard'?"

Amanda Bauer didn't. The softly muttered word that actually came out of her mouth was a lot less welcoming. And had fewer letters. Four, to be exact.

The man shook his head and tsked. "Not exactly the friendly skies. Haven't caught the spirit yet this morning?"

"Make one more airline-slogan crack and you'll be walking to Chicago," she said.

He nodded once, then pushed his sunglasses onto the top of his tousled hair. The move revealed blue eyes that matched the sky above. And yeah. They were twinkling. Damn it.

"Understood. Just, uh, promise me you'll say 'Coffee, tea or me' at least once, okay? Please?"

Amanda tried to glare, but that twinkle sucked the annoyance right out of her. She could only draw in a slow breath as he climbed into the plane. As she watched her passenger disappear into the small jet, she had to wonder about the trip she was about to take.

Coffee and tea they had, and he was welcome to them. But her? Well, she'd never even considered making a move on a customer before. Talk about unprofessional.

And yet…

Something inside her suddenly wanted to take a chance, to be a little outrageous.

How long since she had done indecent things—or decent ones, for that matter—with a sexy man? Not since before they'd thrown all their energies into expanding Clear-Blue Air, at the very least. She hadn't had time for a lunch date, much less the kind of lust-fest she'd enjoyed in her younger years. The kind that lasted for entire weekends and involved not leaving a bed except to grab the kind of sensuous food that could be smeared onto—and eaten off—someone else's hot, naked, sweat-tinged body.

She closed her eyes, her hand clenching tight on the railing. Her heart fluttered in her chest and she tried to make herself move. But she couldn't—not climbing up, but not backing away, either. Not physically, and not in her head.

Was she really considering this? God, she hadn't even looked at the stranger's left hand to make sure he was available. She had no idea if he was actually attracted to her or just an irrepressible flirt. Yet something inside was telling her to take a shot with this man.

It was crazy. Something she'd never considered. Yet right now, at this moment, she was definitely considering it. If he was available…could she do it? Seduce a stranger? Have an anonymous fling, like something out of a blue movie on late-night cable?

She didn't know. All she knew was that the flight to Chicago was a short one so she had to decide quickly. And as she put her foot on the bottom step and began to climb up, Amanda suddenly had to wonder if she was about to embark on the ride of her life.

Do you have a forbidden fantasy?

Amanda Bauer does. She's always craved a life of adventure…sexual adventure, that is. And when she meets Reese Campbell, she knows he's just the man to play with. And play they do. Every few months they get together for days of wild sex, no strings attached—or so they think….

Sneak away with:

Play with Me

by LESLIE KELLY

*Available February 2010
wherever Harlequin books are sold.*

---

red-hot reads

www.eHarlequin.com

HARLEQUIN *Presents*

PREGNANT BRIDES

*Inexperienced and expecting,
they're forced to marry!*

Bestselling Harlequin Presents author

Lynne Graham

brings you the second story
in this exciting new trilogy:

RUTHLESS MAGNATE,
CONVENIENT WIFE
#2892
Available February 2010

Also look for

GREEK TYCOON,
INEXPERIENCED MISTRESS
#2900
Available March 2010

www.eHarlequin.com

HP12892

REQUEST YOUR FREE BOOKS!

2 FREE NOVELS PLUS 2 FREE GIFTS!

HARLEQUIN®

Blaze™

Red-hot reads!

Sold, bought, bargained for or bartered

He'll take his…

Bride on Approval

Whether there's a debt to be paid,
a will to be obeyed or a business
to be saved…she has no choice
but to say, "I do"!

PURE PRINCESS,
BARTERED BRIDE
by *Caitlin Crews*
#2894

Available February 2010!

HARLEQUIN® *Blaze*™

It all started with a few naughty books....

As a member of the Red Tote Book Club, Carol Snow has been studying works of classic erotic literature…but Carol doesn't believe in love…or marriage. It's going to take another kind of classic—Charles Dickens's *A Christmas Carol*—and a little otherworldly persuasion to convince her to go after her own sexily ever after.

Cuddle up with

Her Sexy Valentine

by STEPHANIE BOND

Available February 2010

---

red-hot reads